ANGRY
Management

CHRIS CRUTCHER

Author of *Deadline*

ANGRY
Management

THREE NOVELLAS

Greenwillow Books
An Imprint of HarperCollinsPublishers

Angry Management
Copyright © 2009 by Chris Crutcher

The text of this book is set in ITC Galliard.
Book design by Sylvie Le Floc'h

Lyrics from "A Friend of Mine Is Going Blind" copyright © 1975
by John Dawson Read. Reproduced by permission of the author.

Library of Congress Cataloging-in-Publication Data
Crutcher, Chris.
Angry management / by Chris Crutcher.
p. cm.
"Greenwillow Books."
Summary: A collection of short stories featuring characters
from earlier books by Chris Crutcher.
ISBN 978-0-06-050247-8 (trade bdg.)
— ISBN 978-0-06-050246-1 (lib. bdg.)
[1. Short stories.] I. Title.
PZ7.C89An 2009   [Fic]—dc22   2008052829

09 10 11 12 CG/RRDH First Edition 10 9 8 7 6 5 4 3 2

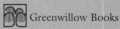
Greenwillow Books

In memory of
Jeremy Salvner

Foreword

I'm not big on writing fantasy, but for the purposes of this trilogy I have stepped over the line and whipped up a bit of magic myself. I'm bringing together characters I created separately over a fifteen-year span. In this book, they've stayed the same ages they were when I created them. Hey, the Hardy Boys have remained teenagers for more than three quarters of a century.

So Sarah Byrnes and Angus Bethune and John Simet and Matt Miller and Montana West are living outside of their original times and in some cases outside of their original settings. If that bothers you, I salute you because it means you've read more than one of my formal novels.

Writing this was a great challenge for me. I'm asked over and over again whether or not there will be a sequel to *Staying Fat for Sarah Byrnes* or *Whale Talk*, or if I'm ever going to write an entire novel in which Angus Bethune stands front and center. I don't know the answer to the last question—Angus could certainly shoulder his own book—but I don't generally get the notion to write a sequel to a novel that I've already taken two years to write. But during those two years I always fall in love with my characters, and I loved revisiting some of them in this other, shorter form.

But *Angry Management* isn't simply a tribute to those characters I love: it's also a tribute to some of my fans. Those who have read *Whale Talk* may remember John Simet as the swimming coach/teacher and mentor to T. J., the main character. I remember Simet quite differently. Not long after my novel *Ironman* was released, I received an e-mail from a student at the University of Nebraska. He referred to several of my novels, and I was taken by his knowledge of their details. At the bottom of the e-mail was his auto-generated homage to the Nebraska Cornhuskers football team. My team was the University of Washington Huskies, and the last time I'd seen the two teams play, the Huskies had killed 'em, and, after thanking him for his generous comments, I mentioned that. Within minutes I received a second e-mail: "They play tomorrow," he wrote. "If UW wins, I'll buy every one of your books in hardback and send you the receipt. If the Cornhuskers win, you have to use my name in a book."

"You're on," I wrote back.

I had not been paying recent attention to college football. The Huskies were on their way *down*, and the Cornhuskers were in the running for the national championship. If I recall correctly, Nebraska beat the Huskies by three touchdowns plus.

When the game was over, I hopped on the computer and e-mailed John. "Do you want to be a freeway sniper or a one-legged transvestite?" I typed.

"I don't care," he wrote back. "Just put my name in a book."

Done.

A name I'm sure you won't remember from reading my books, unless you are a *true* trivia expert, is Matt Miller, whom you will meet, should you read on, in the story "Meet Me at the Gates, Marcus James." Matt Miller had one mention in *Deadline* as a member of the football team—even minor characters would call him minor. But Matt Miller is also a young man who came to a bookstore reading a couple of years back. After the reading he handed me his copy of *Deadline* and asked me to sign it on the page where his name was mentioned. I was so taken with his intelligence and his sense of humor that by the time we finished our conversation, I was determined to give him a bigger role somewhere down the line.

We are down the line, and I give you Matt Miller.

—Chris Crutcher

NAK

Mr. Nak removes books from cardboard boxes and places them in some order that makes sense to him, onto the bookshelves occupying three of the four walls of his small office. There are fiction books, biographies, left-leaning political tomes dating back to the Reagan years. Bronze statues of horses divide sections; framed pictures of his recent first trip to his ancestors' homeland, Japan, hang on the one newly painted eggshell wall, along with his all-around cowboy plaque won in an obscure senior rodeo circuit on the dusty plains of West Texas.

He plops into the oversized office chair and places his boots on the desk, gazing around the room, letting his eyes fall on the rodeo plaque. Fifteen years ago, he left a job much like this one to get back to his Japanese cowboy roots; now he's back. Sixty-two is too damned old to make the lightning trip from saddle to dirt one more time. Symmetry. He nods, grateful that Global Community Health was willing to hire him as a full-time counselor at an age when many counselors retire.

"We have kids in this two-state region who need help, Mr. Nakatani. Our jurisdiction covers three school districts, large in area but not so much in population. Last year was a rough one; we had two suicides—one by gun and one by overdose—and at least one major racial incident. We need to get some prevention going."

"Sounds like the job for me, ma'am," Nak said. "I ain't braggin', but I've worked with kids in tough situations all my life. Been in a few myself. I think your right, getting a jump on 'er, by the way."

"You come highly recommended from your years in the Clark Forks school district, and you'll be working with some of those kids. But we're expanding our embrace, if you will. Some of the grant money for your salary was written for kids who aren't in the direst of straits; kids who have run into some hard luck or ones with a fragile emotional makeup. You know, kids who will make it if they get a chance to work some things through," Dr. Hairston said. "I'll make sure you have whatever you need."

"'Preciate it."

That was it. Shortest interview he'd ever had.

Two suicides, a major racial incident, plus the various and sundry stuff kids go through to get to graduation. Hopefully.

World's dangerous enough without bringing your

own firearm to your head, or your mother's prescription pills to your gut.

Nak thumbs through his list of possible clients; the terminally tough crowd first, then the kids recently graduated or ready to graduate that Dr. Hairston thinks could use a little boost. He was impressed when he read Global Community Health's mission statement. It was the first preventative program he'd read about that might be worth its salt, and the first that seemed adventurous enough to work with clients' real lives. He appreciated that they worked with and through the school districts. This seems like a good place to wrap things up.

Sarah Byrnes, Angus Bethune, Montana West (some of these names sounded like they were concocted by a bad fiction writer), Matt Miller (that's a little more like it), Trey Chase. Sixteen names in all.

"We've separated these kids into two groups, one with kids we think can fly and one with kids who desperately need survival skills. Once you meet them, you may want to move them around, but that's all up to you. It's your program, Mr. Nakatani, we think we have the best man for the job."

He looks at the header on their stationery. IF YOU THINK YOUR LIFE SUCKS, IT PROBABLY DOES. DO SOMETHING ABOUT IT.

Global Community Health has done a hell of a job selling their wares, Nak thinks.

"My name's Noboru Nakatani. My few friends call me Nobi, or Nak. You can put Mister in front of that if your so moved, but I got no requirement. The folks runnin' this rodeo think all y'all can learn to ride; sit tall in the saddle, to use a metaphor I'm comfortable with, so I'm here to help you find the right saddle and bridle. I know some of y'all don't know each other, and none of ya know me, so we can start slow, but in the end if ya want to make things work, ya got to tell your story and ya got to tell it true.

"I call this group Angry Management. I call all my groups Angry Management. Tell ya why. Back in the day I worked with a young man named Hudge. Kid had one of the nastiest daddies I know about; that boy operated his whole life in the eye of a particularly vicious hurricane. Least a category five. Kid's brain wadn't operatin' on much horsepower, if you know what I mean, an' he was scared all the damn time, for good reason."

Nak shakes his head, slides back in time. "Forgot to feed his dog one mornin', so his ol' man *killed* the dog, then told Hudge *he'd* killed him. His dad had warned Hudge when he asked to have a dog that he would have to care for him an' he damn well better not forget or there would be consequences." Nak looks toward the window. "That man could lay down some *consequences.*

"It was Valentine's Day, first one ever where ol' Hudge stood a good chance to get one. Got all fixed up, combed his hair; even put on a little deodorant—an' forgot to feed the damn dog. Only time he forgot in three years. The ol' man shot that dog. Laid him right there on the porch so Hudge couldn't miss him when he come home." Nak looks at his boots. "Hell, ol' Hudge tore up the two valentines he got 'cause he blamed wantin' 'em for makin' him forget, then got so damn mad he tried to pull off his own skin."

Nak looks around the circle of kids in this first group. "Like I said, Hudge wadn't all that articulate. The group I had 'im in was called Anger Management. Hudge couldn't quite get it, called it Angry Management. State took Hudge away an' tried to find 'im a foster home, but that didn't work out, so they found 'im a residential treatment center. Guess that didn't work out either, 'cause ol' Hudge took himself out. That boy hanged himself in a coat closet." Nak looks directly into the eyes of all who can hold his gaze. "The kid was a real hero to make it as far as he did. I call all my groups Angry Management in his name; make sure I won't forget him. So welcome to Angry Management.

"I want to get to know your stories. I want all y'all to know each *other's* stories, because if we can work us up a little trust, we can probably help each other out.

"We got the Vegas rule, and I hit this one hard. What happens here, *stays* here. There ain't a lot of things you can do to get the boot, but takin' what's said here out to the teemin' masses is one of 'em. That's one I need a promise on, so I'll send this here paper around the room and I'd appreciate it if you'd put your John Hancock on it."

Trey Chase: "What's a John Hancock? Isn't that your . . . you know . . . dick?"

"No, that's usually your Johnson. You'll have to bear with me. I'm an old guy. A John Hancock is your signature. You got to sign the paper."

Every kid in this group is a volunteer. Every kid in this group wants to fly. Every kid in this group has too much ballast. The paper circulates, stopping at Trey. He reads it over.

Montana West leans over. "Sign it and quit pretending you can read."

He smiles, signs. "I'd follow you through fire."

"I like a good-looking boy with below-average intelligence," she says back.

Angus Bethune says, "Let's get some *heft* on this

paper" and snatches it from Trey; signs with flair, the pen nearly disappearing in his beefy hand.

"Since this is the first session," Nak says, "I'll tell you a little bit about myself and then answer as many of your questions as I can, and maybe get a statement from you out of the gate.

"I used to be a teacher. B'fore that I was a kid, just like you. Last time I received instruction in a high school, it was 1964. That's back during evolution for you, but it's yesterday to me. They tell me this area went down a hard road last year, and they pulled me in to see if I could get a little prevention goin'. In my world that's a good idea; ever town that cares about its youngsters should do it. Anyway, the reason I'm good at this job, and I am good at it, is 'cause I've been down a shit . . . er . . . hard road or two of my own, an' I'm still standin'."

Matt Miller says, "It's okay to say shit, Mr. Nak. "I'm the Christian boy in here, and I say it all the time."

"Christian boy says I can say it, I can say it," Nak says. "I don't expect y'all to tell your stories yet. You'll have to learn to trust each other first, an' then me. In the end, my hope is that you'll learn that Angry Management ain't really where it's at. When the rage has got ya, it's got ya. But if you learn to tell your story, an' tell it loud, your angry won't get you so often. Any questions?"

····
7

CHRIS CRUTCHER

Marcus James raises his hand. "This group equal opportunity?"

"Meanin'?"

Marcus looks around. "Well, you might not have noticed, but I'm the only black guy here."

"You might not have noticed, but I'm the only Japanese guy here," Nak says. "Got you covered."

"Well, I'm probably the only gay guy here, too," Marcus says.

Nak looks around. "Hard to tell. But I'm probably the only cowboy here, so, like I say, got you covered." He nods. "Any more questions?"

There are none.

"Well, I'm your best friend today, 'cause I'm lettin' you out early. Go git your stories straight. Let's call 'er a day."

Nak's Notes
First Impressions
Transcribed directly from digital recorder

NAME: *Sarah Byrnes*

AGE: *18*

REASONS TO BE PISSED: *Abused by Daddy, abandoned by Momma. Disfigured in a way she can't hide. Suffered taunts of peers throughout educational career; few if any chances to love or be loved physically.*

COPING SKILLS: *Defensive, keeps to own self. Mess with her and she'll kick your ass.*

SIGNIFICANT CHARACTERISTICS: *Low expectations of others, covers most emotions with simmering anger. Good physical condition. Smart as hell. Possible sense of humor. Truly tough enough to kick your ass.*

PROGNOSIS: *Dang. Who knows?*

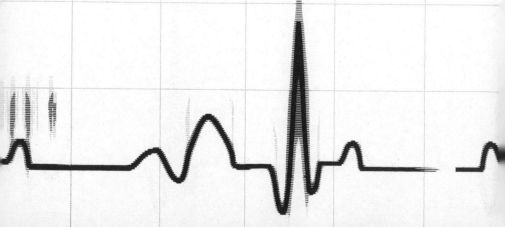

NAME: *Angus Bethune*

AGE: *18*

REASONS TO BE PISSED: *Parents and stepparents in well-publicized non-traditional relationship that coils around itself like a bunch of rattlesnakes huddlin' from the cold, which he tends to defend with a quick punch to the gut. Big guy. Hard to hide. Not much experience with the ladies.*

COPING SKILLS: *Witty; great sense of humor. History indicates that, past a point, he's toting a big-time temper.*

SIGNIFICANT CHARACTERISTICS: *Likely to speak before thinking. Self-esteem lower than a snake's belly. Smart as a whip. Funny. Good athlete. Empathetic. Good parents, but man, some of them seem clueless.*

PROGNOSIS: *Same.*

Kyle Maynard
and the Craggy Face of the Moon

I load another thirty-five-pound weight onto each side of the bench press bar and take a deep breath. A girl I recognize waits patiently a few steps away. I sit, smile at her, but she looks away.

"You waiting for this?" I ask. "I have a bunch of other machines I need to use, and they're in no particular order."

"Go ahead," she says back. I can use the breather."

"You're Sarah, right? From Mr. Nak's group?"

"Hard to pick me out, huh?" she says facetiously, pointing to the burn scars on her face.

I slap my forehead. "Yeah. Duh."

She looks away.

"I'm Angus," I tell her, slapping my prodigious gut.

"At least as easy to remember as you. They named me after a cow."

"I can go you one better," Sarah says back. "My last name is Byrnes." She pronounces it Burns.

"Jesus, that's like if they named me Angus Fat."

"You're too kind."

"Duh! Again. I didn't mean—"

"Sure you did. I'm scarred and you're fat and that's why we work out in the relative anonymity of four-thirty in the morning."

I glance around the large facility, from the free-weight area to the weight machines to the empty treadmills and elliptical machines facing TV screens. If an infomercial plays on a TV screen no one is watching, will someone still buy stupid shit? "There are a couple of guys over there who look pretty good," I tell her, nodding toward the leg press, "and the girl on the bike could be worse. It isn't all just us Frankensteins."

Sarah looks at the cyclist. "You into thongs?"

"Can't afford to be," I say. "I never saw anyone in a thong looking for a whale ride."

She stares at the girl a moment more, plugs her earphones back into her Nano, and shrugs. "Better get back to this."

I nod, knowing she can no longer hear me, and

mumble, "Maybe you want to get a cup of coffee with me sometime?" I lie back on the bench.

"Maybe," she says.

I spring up. She waves the Nano. "Between songs," she says. "Wanna take it back?"

"Nope. Wanna pretend you didn't hear?"

"Nope."

"So tell us a little more about this girl. You say she's been burned?" Alexander says over his salad. My parents and their mates and I are spending the evening, as we do every second Wednesday, at the Extended Family Solidarity Dinner. I rate it: B+ food; zero social value.

"Yeah, a little bit burned. She's, you know, kind of straightforward—okay, *way* straightforward—but a good personality. Works out."

"And you're going on a date?" Mom seems a little too incredulous.

"It's just coffee, but yeah, Mom, a date. I'm eighteen."

"And you've been on one date," Dad says.

"Well, if this one works out and I have one more, it'll be a trifecta," I say. "Jeez, take a breath."

"We're breathing, we're breathing," Dad says. His name is Orville. "We just want to know that she's . . . you know."

"Good enough for me?"

"We're your parents, Angus. We'll never stop worrying."

I glance at Bella, sipping from her wine glass, clear of the fray. "What do you think, Bella?"

She smiles. "I think a boy should listen to his mother."

"Which one of you is my mother again?" I survey the crew, halt my conversation as the waitress sets the He-Man T-Bone before me. "Since kindergarten I've been explaining to my very few friends that I have four parents, all gay as court jesters and all living on the same city block." I rise into falsetto.

"'So, like, Angus, one of those guys is your dad and he's, like, kind of married to the other guy? What do you call *that* guy?'"

And in an altered falsetto, my own younger voice, "'I call him Alexander.'

"'Yeah, but what do you *call* him, like your step-homo?'

"'I call him Alexander, asshole,'" and I smack my fist into my palm.

"I do seem to remember you explaining our situation with your fists on occasion," Mom says.

"My point," I say back, "is that I have a Ph.D. in

observing exotic relationships, so I guess I can be trusted to pick one strange enough to keep you all happy."

"My god," Dad says. "You're serious about this girl. What's her name?"

"Her name is Sarah, and I'm having *coffee* with her. Tap your helmet, Dad."

Mom says, "Well, it's about time, that's all I can say."

If only that were true.

"Worst thing that ever happened to you." Sarah adds nonfat milk to her coffee, removes a scone from that tissue-y paper bag they give you. She looks around the rustic coffeehouse that is Rocket Bakery. "Beats Starbucks."

"Worst thing. Lemme see." I pull out my frosted pumpkin scone, place it next to my banana bread. "They hoisted my undershorts up the flagpole during gym class in junior high. Totally blotted out the Stars and Stripes. Probably not the worst thing, but it comes to mind when I'm asked that. Guys used to leave bras in my locker, but that wasn't so bad. I just took them home and . . . never mind."

"If we're going to be married, I have to trust you," Sarah says.

"We're getting married?"

"We're on a date, aren't we? You know what that leads to. So, if I'm going to trust you, you have to tell the truth. Worst thing, not worst funny thing."

"You drive a hard bargain. You have, like, our dishes picked out?"

"Worst thing."

"Maybe sitting with my mother when she was so depressed she couldn't move. You know, trying to cheer her up when all she could do was sit and stare; tears she didn't even feel streaming down her cheeks."

"What was going on?"

"Ah, you know. Junior high. I was getting into it on a regular basis when some kid would call my parents queer or faggots or whatever. If I'd have just told the teachers, the other kid would've gotten in trouble, but I liked to avoid the middle man back then; I *hurt* some guys. So Mom and Dad came to school for this big meeting. Two teachers, the principal, two kids who still had black eyes, with their parents, and them. I got labeled armed and dangerous. Dad kept telling them school was supposed to be a safe place for me, and they said it *was* safe if I'd just report what was happening instead of taking the law into my own hands. The parents of wounded Thing One and Thing

Two said what about *their* kids' safety, and I took the opportunity to let them know exactly how their kids could keep themselves safe."

Sarah almost spits her coffee.

"Guess I should have practiced the delivery, because when the meeting was over I was on two months in-school suspension and the other *parents* were calling mine faggots and queers."

"Sounds like a meeting or two I've been in."

"Yeah. So my mother talks all the way home about how their lifestyle has ruined me and how she and Dad should have stayed in the closet until I graduated from high school. Dad gave her his Hallmark bullshit about the truth setting us free, and she got quieter and quieter. Dad went home to Alexander and Mom went home to Bella and everyone warned me not to kick any more asses, which I promised I wouldn't—just like I promised every time—and Mom started the Big Retreat. I would come home after school and sit with her and try to convince her she hadn't fucked up my life. It was like talking to a bag of rocks. She just kept sinking."

"So what brought her out of it?"

"Time, I guess. As much as I wanted to save her while I sat by her side, that disappeared when some kid would turn the crank on my temper. So I turned out for football in high school and started taking out my rage on unsuspecting offensive linemen and running backs. I was pretty good; made a few friends. Mom finally figured out I'd survive, and they went on living their lives."

Sarah says, "That's more like it."

"More like what?"

"Truth. I asked for the worst thing. That was pretty good."

"That's off the top of my head. Let me think about it a while; maybe I can top it."

"That's good enough for now," she says.

I walk to the counter for refills and order two thick slices of banana bread and two more scones, remember my manners, and turn back to her. "You want anything else to eat?"

She looks at me pitifully, shakes her head, and pats her stomach.

"I like that," I tell her when I sit back down with my goodies. "Keepin' your girlish figger."

"Like that's ever done me any good." She stares in mock wonder as I lay out my repast. "What's your cholesterol count?"

I count. "Two banana breads, two scones. Four."

"You're my second fat boy."

"Seriously? Awright! You'll know how to treat me."

"With great disdain. His name was Moby."

"Like the whale. Does he fit in on the question *you* now have to answer?"

"What question is that?"

"The worst thing that ever happened to you."

"Indeed he does," she says. "Sure you want to hear this?"

"Not if you're going to tell me you're going back to the other fat guy."

She laughs. "Actually, he's not fat anymore; at least not *way* fat. And I was never *with* him. He was my friend, and he probably saved my life."

"That's fair. *Way* fat, huh?"

"I didn't mean . . . "

"Yeah you did," I say, taking in the carbohydrate circus in front of me. "Maybe I should get to know this guy." I put a napkin over the food. "Let's see if I can get through your story without scarfing these." I sit back. "Okay. Worst thing."

This *has* to be about her scars, and I'm not sure I want to hear it. There's something beguiling about this girl. She *is* disfigured, and as much as I'd like to be bigger than that (hell, I'm bigger than almost everything else), I'm not sure how it affects me. Without my glasses, which I only wear when I *need* to see, she's blurred at the edges, and I see a beauty, a femininity that doesn't hide behind her toughness, probably because she doesn't know it's there. And I gotta tell you, I know what it's like to not quite pass muster on looks.

"I don't know how much I remember and how much I imagine," Sarah says. "I was young; three or four. Pretty, everyone says. I remember being so scared of my dad. I'd see him through the window coming home from work and I'd stand just around the kitchen entrance and wait to see if he was dangerous that day. I'd watch my mother. I could tell how he was by her shoulders. If he was in a good mood—and good is relative here—her shoulders slumped and I could *feel* the relief; if he was mean they would pinch up high around her neck. When they slumped, I'd come around into the kitchen and wait to see if I got a hug. It wasn't much of a hug, like nothing to *sustain* you, but if I got anything, we were safe for the night.

"Then it seemed like the slumped shoulders and hugs just disappeared. When I look back, I know he was drinking more, because we'd have to wait longer for him to come home to dinner. You didn't eat *anything* before he got there."

It scares me even to hear it. "How crazy was this guy?"

"As crazy as he still is," she says. "But don't judge him yet. It gets better."

"I thought so."

"My mother would cook dinner so it would be ready when he got home, and he'd come late and fly into a rage because dinner was cold. So she'd wait for him, and he'd fly into a rage because dinner wasn't on the table. I remember it because every night she would ask me what I thought she should do. I wouldn't know, so I'd make a guess and she'd do it. It was like living your life at a roulette wheel with no colors or numbers. You couldn't pick a winner because even when you did time it right, the food still had to be something he liked."

"I've played roulette," I tell her. "There's almost no chance to pick a winner when there *are* numbers or colors."

"Well, you had a hell of a lot better chance than we had. And losing *really* sucked. Swear to god, my clearest memory of my mother is the smack of his hand against her head."

"Why didn't she just take you and leave?"

"Looking for the answer to that question will keep therapists in work for eternity. Anyway, one night the stars lined up exactly wrong. He was at the door and then he and my mother were screaming and then he had her by the hair and the water was running in the sink and he was pushing her face into the water, 'You can't talk if you can't breathe, bitch,' and I was scared but I was *mad* and I ran at him and started bashing his legs with my fists, screaming at him to leave her alone and then I was in his arms and the potbelly stove was coming right at my face and then this awful, like, *searing* pain and I was screaming and then we were back in the kitchen. He pushed me at her and said, 'There's your pretty little girl for you.'

"Next thing I remember, I *think*, was pitch dark, because my face was covered with bandages. Hands, too, where I put them out to stop the stove. I heard my dad telling nurses I had pulled a kettle of boiling spaghetti over on myself when my mom wasn't looking. I still don't know how in the world anyone bought that bullshit because a scalding burn and a dry burn are *way* different, but it was a small town and people don't get into other people's business, even doctors, and no one ever called child protection. I don't even know if there was suspicion. My dad was meaner than a snake, but he could turn on 'earnest' anytime."

I am glued to her.

She sips her coffee. "Like I said, I'm not sure how much I remember exactly and how much I made up.

Some of it I heard again at my dad's trial last year. I was *young*. For a long time I believed the story about the spaghetti, because he told it over and over and so did my mom. It was easier to believe than the truth. But when it came back, it was like it was happening right then."

"Jesus, my worst thing would be your best thing."

She smiles. "I'm not to the worst thing yet."

Jesus.

"When I got home from the hospital, I stayed close to my mother. If she left the room, I howled; followed her everywhere I could. But it was like she wasn't in there. I mean, she let me tag along through our tiny place, but she didn't talk, didn't sing to me anymore, or tell me how much she loved me. Nothing. She moved like a ghost, and I followed her like a ghost, but she was my mom and I couldn't stand to have any distance between us. There was no more fighting. Dad came home and didn't say a word, and my mother would figure out some way to get his dinner. He ate alone. She fed me before he got there."

Sarah sighs, and I swear there isn't a breath between us, but there are crumbs because I'm not holding to my dietary pledge. She shakes her head like a dog clearing its ears, bringing herself into the moment. "*Here's* the worst thing," she says.

"It's night. My mom is home and Dad isn't. I hear her crashing around upstairs in her room. I run up and see her throwing clothes into two suitcases on the bed, stuffing them in. I stand in the doorway and she doesn't see me, just packs faster and faster. I say, 'Are you throwing stuff away?' and she sees me and gasps, then keeps packing. 'Are you?' I say. She kneels in front of me. 'Listen, Sarah, I have to go away' and I say, 'No!' 'I have to,' she says, and I say, 'I'm coming, too.' She says, 'I have to go alone,' and I start to cry. '*I'm coming, too!*' She shakes me. 'I'll come back and get you. I have to get us a place to live,' and I yell 'No! No! No!'

"I hear a car horn and run to the window. The car is yellow. I'm screaming and holding on to her, so she says, 'Okay, okay! Run and get your clothes. Hurry. Use the play suitcase I bought you. Get a dress and some underpants. Bring your bear. Hurry, your dad is coming.' I run like the wind to my room, get my favorite dress and a pair of pants and a shirt. I stuff in some underpants and I look all around but I can't find my bear and I'm so scared to leave it and I'm trying to hurry. I dig in the closet, and then I hear a car door slam and I panic. My heart *pounds* in my ears, and I run to the window in time to see a leg disappearing into the backseat, with my mother's shoe on it. I scream at the window, but it's closed and no one looks up and the yellow car drives away."

I'm so lost in this I've almost stopped eating. "A cab. *Please* tell me she came back."

"She came back."

Ahhh. "Really?"

"Nope. You said to tell you that."

"She didn't."

The next time I saw her was in Reno, thirteen years later."

"Reno? Nevada?"

"You know another Reno?"

I don't.

"In grade school I got these postcards from there. No writing, just pictures of casinos and shows and stars who sang there. The casinos looked like castles. I dreamed the postcards were from my mother and when the time was right she would come get me to go live in one of the castles with her. My friend, Moby, the other fat guy, figured out when we were in high school that they *had* to be from her, and this teacher, Ms. Lemry, risked her job to take me there to find her."

I look at the crumbs on the table in front of me. I'm thinking maybe the other fat guy wouldn't have eaten them, which was why he was no longer the other fat guy.

Sarah breaks me out of my dietary reverie. "We found her."

"You found her? You're not saying that because you heard me thinking, Please tell me you found her."

"We found her. She was a waitress at a restaurant in one of those casinos on the postcards. My teacher recognized the shame on her face when she saw a burned girl sitting in the booth, plus I had one *way* old picture. There couldn't have been one chance in a million we'd find her, but there's less chance than that to win the lottery and somebody always does. Anyway, she knew it was me somehow, and she tried to run, but Ms. Lemry chased her down. My mother sat right there in the middle of the street and refused to come back . . . said she knew she would rot in hell, but she was scareder than she was ashamed."

I am pushing my finger into the last crumbs on the table, eating them slowly, trying to wrap my imagination around all this. "So losing your mother is a worse thing than getting burned?"

"You never get used to losing your mom," she says. "I hate her. I mean, I *hate* her. I hate her worse than my dad, but I'd give anything to have her back, even if it was just to tell her to go to hell."

Wow. "Where's your dad?"

"Prison," she says. "It's amazing. He raised me and we had a *few* times that were okay, but I don't care if I never see him again. She knew what he was like and she *left* me with him, but I *ache* to be with her sometimes. It's *so* crazy. Maybe I just want her to know how much I hate her, but in my dreams . . . that's not it. I don't get it; most times I hate myself for wanting her."

I sit, digesting her story, and the scones. I remember hating my own parents because they were gay and wouldn't shut up about it. I hated them every time some kid brought it up or asked out loud how I thought I might have been conceived, and then described the possibilities. But my parents were *always* there. The one thing I've always counted on, come hell or high water, was that they were looking out for me. Maybe I was embarrassed by them, but by now I know that's *my* problem. I live in two different houses with people I have to explain, but my back is covered, and those people love me like I'm the only kid in the world.

"It did help to get to see her that one time. She's weak. It feels good to know she's weak; that it wasn't me."

"So she looked you in the eye and . . . "

" . . . said no. I needed her to come tell what he'd done. No way could I prove it in court after living with him all that time. I'd never let on to him that I remembered what really happened. I stuck with the spaghetti story. But he seemed crazier and crazier, wondering if I'd figured it out and was waiting to get far enough away to tell. I needed my mother to come put him away. She said she was too scared, but I think the other part was that she would've had to come back and face the shame of leaving me with him."

"So how did your dad get caught?"

"He got crazy when I ran off to Reno, thinking the jig was up, and he went after Moby to find out where I'd gone. Moby wouldn't tell and he got violent and Moby's stepdad hunted him down."

My jealousy surprises me. This other fat guy not only went Jenny Craig on me; he, like, saved Sarah's life. "So this Moby, are you sure you guys weren't . . . you know."

"No. We weren't you know."

"Why not?"

"Look at me, you dick. Besides, he liked a prom queen. And even though he got all buff, I remembered him as the dweeb he was when I met him."

I am looking at her—my glasses are in the car—and she looks *fine*. I've been running around after pretty girls all my life, and to understate it a little, it *hasn't been working*. Something crazy is going on inside me. "How'd he lose the weight?"

"Well, he didn't eat four scones with every cup of coffee. And he turned out for swimming."

I brush the crumbs off the table. "*That's* not fair. I was a football player."

"I kind of owe him everything, but that's about what he owes me, so it's even."

"Swimming, huh?"

"It's not for everyone."

At three-thirty in the morning, an hour before Sarah usually gets here, I sign in to 24-Hour Fitness. There's only one other person here, if you don't count the girl behind the counter and the guy running the vacuum and washing mirrors. Mirrors are the one thing I'd have taken out of this place if I ran the zoo.

In the dressing room I take a swimming suit out of my workout bag that was designed for Shrek. Man, how did this Moby guy get through those first days swimming? At some point he would have had to don a swimming suit of similar design and hit the water, in front of an entire swimming team. Gutsy dude.

I pull on the suit, reach under my gut to tie it, throw an extra-wide-body beach towel around my shoulders, and make my way to the pool. No *way* is anyone here ahead of me.

Someone's here ahead of me. And she is not the person I want witnessing the maiden launch of Tugboat Angus. She is like an arrow—an arrow with breasts—and could make four of the suits she's wearing from my one. She stands under the showerhead stretching, touching her toes; looks up to catch me staring, smiles, and reaches for her toes again. It's too late to run, so I walk onto the deck like I'm not afraid it will give way under my poundage, clutching my towel like Superman headed into a deep freeze.

I stand, goggles in hand, waiting for her to choose a lane and get her head underwater where she can't watch Mr. Goodyear dive in and empty the pool.

Only she isn't a swimmer. She's an aqua jogger.

The reason I believe in God is so I can curse Him. And I know God's a man, by the way, because no way a woman would put me through the stuff I go through. Aqua joggers *run* in the water. Their heads do not go under it. She hauls out the Styrofoam dumbbells and resistance paddles, hops into lane one, and begins jogging toward the other end, head high, only one lane removed from the spectacle that will be my entry.

I curse the Lord God once more, drop the towel,

and lunge. The slim beauty next to me almost loses her balance in the wave action as the lane separators undulate to the far end of the pool and back. I adjust my goggles and start the first lap of what I generously call swimming, vowing to hunt this Moby dude down like the dog he is.

"Let's go find her."

"Been there, done that," Sarah says.

"Yeah, but like you said, she was afraid to come back because your dad was still on the loose. You said he's in prison till he's a bona fide geezer. You don't even have to bring her back now. I mean, look, she had to feel ambushed when you guys showed up that first time, but she's seen you now. You've seen her. We can go back to Reno and get all your questions answered."

"What you need to worry about is taking me someplace besides to coffee," she says. "If you don't take me on a real date pretty soon, people will start to believe you think I'm ugly."

Man, you get nothing past this girl. When my eyes go soft—like out of focus—or with no glasses, there's nothing ugly about her, but she's right; I've been avoiding going on a real date. I tell myself it's not because she's scarred, and I believe that. It's that I'm scared I'll blow it with her like I've done in spectacular fashion with every girl I ever allowed into my weirdball fantasies. Sarah Byrnes has so much . . . *substance*. When I first see her, the scars are evident. But then they disappear the minute we're talking. Jesus, maybe I'm getting mature.

"A date it is," I tell her. "Circus Circus. Coupons for free breakfast and a roll of nickels to play the slots. Yours with no questions asked. What happens in Reno, stays in Reno. I've got superb wheels, thanks to my parents' collective guilt; we could be there in two days easy. Drive straight through, we could do it in one. You drive, right?"

"Yes, Angus, I drive."

"That's it then," I tell her. "I'll even let you plug *your* iPod into the radio."

"This must be what love feels like." Man, this girl has sarcastic *down*. But she didn't say no. We'll miss one of Mr. Nak's groups, but shit, we should get extra credit for this.

There is such excitement building in me. Crazy as my life has seemed, if I lost either of my parents the way Sarah lost hers, I don't know that I could stand up every day. I want her to feel better. I'm telling you, having parents that love you trumps everything, even I know that.

■ ■ ■

We're shooting through the Palouse, past rolling wheat fields, about a hundred miles south of Spokane, near the Idaho border where Washington State University and the University of Idaho play Dueling Universities just nine miles apart. Sarah is supposed to go to WSU in the fall; I'm headed for U of I. Nine miles apart; could be worse.

"If I say turn around, we turn around," Sarah says.

"Aye aye, Captain."

"I'm serious, Angus."

"Do I look dumb enough to keep going if you tell me to turn around? Don't answer that. But I'm serious, too. If you say turn around, I'll show you true stunt-driver action."

"Even if I say it at the Reno city limits."

"Even if you say it at the front door of the restaurant," I say back. "Even if you say it when we're sitting in the booth."

"If you're just saying that, and you think you'll figure some way to change my mind if it happens, I'll punch your stomach so hard your *cousins* will double over."

"Man, that other fat guy must have been a deceiver of the first order."

She's quiet a minute. "That other fat guy did play fast and loose with the truth on occasion."

"Not all fat guys are alike."

"All guys are alike," she says. And then, "All humans are alike." She plugs her Nano into the radio and turns the sound high enough that I know to shut up. It's a beautiful day, cool for midsummer, hot for any other time, and the contrast between fields and deep blue sky is so stark we seem like figures in a masterpiece. Words begin to stream through the speakers.

A friend of mine is going blind
But through the dimness,
He sees so much better than me.
And how he cherishes each new thing that he sees
They are locked in his head
He will save them for when
He's in darkness again.

"Who is that?"

"John Dawson Read."

"Who?"

"Old guy. English. You wouldn't know him."

"He's good," I say.

"He's better if you shut up and listen." She flashes a smile.

"Going blind, huh? There's a thought."

"What?"

"Nothing. He's singing about a guy going blind."

We cruise along the Salmon River outside Riggins, Idaho, a little past noon, watching river rafters looking like cool-dude astronauts in their thick life jackets and sunglasses, bucking the light rapids. By late afternoon we're just south of Boise, and finally I've jerked awake enough times that I'm getting whiplash, so I pull over to let her drive.

We've not talked a lot—Sarah doesn't have that need to fill the lapses in conversation, and I'm wondering what we're heading into. The closer we get to Reno, the more remote she seems. We hit the Nevada border in the dark, me blinking in and out of sleep, Sarah with her eyes glued to the road. My glasses are on the dashboard and she is completely beautiful to me, her blurred features smooth in the dim dash lights. I see what would have been, but for a fit of rage. I wonder how much of her personality has been shaped by people's reactions, by not looking into that store window for fear of seeing herself, or wondering if those people crossing the street a half block up are crossing because they really have something to do over there or because they don't want to walk past her.

How does a man do that to a child? What is there

in being human that allows that? Can you imagine pressing a three-year-old girl against a hot wood stove? I get it that he was drunk, but he still had to *do* it. He picked her up and walked to that stove. I've consumed enough alcohol in a sitting to put me over the limit and under the table; hugged the commode like it was the last lifeboat on the *Titanic*. And I've been pissed. I've said things to people I would've taken back in a *second*, were I given the opportunity. I've punched guys for calling my parents names, and I've punched guys for calling me fat or embarrassing me in front of people. I suppose you could say that's on the continuum to doing the kind of damage he did, but on a scale of one to ten, mine is a 0.0003 and his is a sixty. Plus, if I'd ever done anything close to that, I'd kill myself. How do you live with the shame of burning a little girl?

And how in *hell* do you live with the shame of leaving that girl with the guy who burned her? How do you live with yourself after you tricked a terrified little kid into running to her room to get her stuff while you made a clean getaway? Offer her a glimpse of a chance to escape the desperation with you, only to leave her crying at the window. I fucking *know* her mother looked back up at that window. I know it. If I were Sarah, I wouldn't know who to hate either. Man,

I've eaten some shit in my life, but compared to what Sarah has tasted, my shit tasted like angel food cake.

"How much for two rooms?"

"Two-twenty a night," the woman behind the front desk at Harrah's says.

"Do we get free movies and a private masseuse with that?" I ask her.

"Are you being smart with me?"

"Yes, ma'am, I am. Sorry. Do you mind if we huddle?"

I'm eighteen and so is Sarah. Consenting adults.

We sit on a couch amid the din of bells and buzzers announcing jackpots of unimagined size, people moving through the place in a herd, curses. "Look," I tell her, "it's been awhile since you were here. If she doesn't work at the same place, we might have a tough time finding her. We need to conserve our funds. Why don't we get a room with two beds?"

She hesitates a second, says, "Okay."

That was easier than I thought. "We might have to tell them we're married. I don't know. I've never done this before."

"This is Reno, remember?" Sarah says. "What happens in Reno, stays in Reno? You could bring your favorite sheep in here and they wouldn't stop you unless she shits on the floor."

"We decided we want one room," I tell the nice woman behind the desk. "Two double beds."

"What happens in Reno, stays in Reno," she says, looking from me to Sarah and back, thinking, I'm sure, what could possibly happen in Reno between a 270-pound man-child and a crispy child-woman.

"All right then," I say. "Process us in." I peel off six twenties from my roll and hand them over, hoping there'll be a day when I can do that without the pit of my stomach falling out.

"She said two double beds." I stare at the king-sized Sleep Number bed covering about three-quarters of the floor space. I know it's a Sleep Number because there's a sign on the bed that says so, encouraging us to order one off sleepnumber.com if we like it *or*, for just a little less, we could buy a condo. "I'll call down and see if they can put us in a different room."

I pick up the phone as Sarah sits on the bed. She bounces it a couple of times while I wait. "Hang up," she says.

"They haven't answered."

"Drop the phone."

I do.

"I'll bet they don't have these beds in every room. Sit here and check this out."

I walk over and push on it with my hands.

She says, "Sit."

I sit. Whoa! The Sleep Number bed has my number. I fall back and stretch my arms out, like Jesus on that last bad day, minus His discomfort. "Amazing."

"We might not get one if we change rooms," she says.

"There's only one bed."

With her finger she draws a line down the middle and says, "Cross that line and die."

"Right," I say, "and besides, we probably don't have the same sleep number."

"Let's unpack."

I'm sleeping with a *girl* tonight.

My parents brought me to Reno about eight years ago, but it was a whole different experience. They were walking down the sidewalk four abreast, holding hands with me trailing as far back as possible. The sidewalks on the Strip are wide, but you haven't seen wide until you've seen my biological parents. People were walking over the tops of cars to get around them. I spent the night shrugging. People would gawk at them, then back at me, and I'd just shrug, like, who the hell are they?

My parents told me in the old days how dangerous it was to come out of the closet, how often they'd been threatened or belittled. They were so happy to be here in Reno where no one knew them, they couldn't keep their hands off each other. Well, even though prejudice against gays and lesbians has been on the decrease since Ellen DeGeneres smiled sweetly and told the world to kiss her ass, it ain't *all* gone, and I still take my share of hits for having parents so far to the left on the bell-shaped sexual curve. So I just tried to stay below the radar that night.

But now it's Sarah and me walking down the strip and she's burned and I'm fat and it's possible I'm feeling a little of the release my parents felt here. I grab her hand.

She doesn't punch me in the gut.

"Think we should look for her tonight?"

Sarah bumps me with her shoulder, a little aggressively. "Let's do it tomorrow. Last time Ms. Lemry and I caught her on the morning shift in a restaurant in the Sands. Let's take a time out for now."

"You're not sure you're going to do this, are you?" I ask. "The deal is still on, you know. Say the word, and we're burning rubber outta here."

"I need to sleep on it. I'll know in the morning."

We crawl into bed in our sweats. The lights are off but for the dim glow of the TV. Sarah draws the line down the middle of the bed again, though she's laughing. Her side. My side. Never the twain . . . all that. It reminds me of those stories I used to read about the Puritans or some other way too uptight folks "bundling" before marriage. The groom- and bride-to-be would put a board down the middle of the bed, get in with their clothes on, and rack out. It was supposed to be a test; see if they could reign in their horns and prove they believed sex was for procreation only. The way I'm thinking now, I'd have been feeling along that board for the knothole.

Sleeping in one's sweats is not the order of the day for a man of Bethunian girth. I carry my own down covers under my skin and if I bundle, I sweat. We're not talking minor seepage. We're talking rain.

When I think she's asleep, I slip off my sweatshirt ever so carefully, then my sweatpants. Monster boxers I can handle. I crowd the edge of the bed, a good foot from Neverland.

The twain meet. Sometime in the middle of the night, her foot touches my calf. Innocent enough; she's facing the other way. I push my calf into the pressure. Her toe runs up to the back of my knee.

I cannot recount the sequence of events, I don't care to remember the details, lest I discover some *way* crazy indiscretion I committed, like maybe she was asleep except for her foot, and I took advantage. But somehow her sweats end up in a monster wad at the bottom of the bed with mine. I don't know how to proceed, and she doesn't either, but evolution takes over.

I won't speak a word of it. Our secret dies here. I don't know if it was good sex or bad sex, because those terms are relative so you have to do it at least twice to get a measuring stick . . . I mean, *standard*. I only know that when it's over, everything I thought about her, and most of what I thought about myself, is changed. Not like some huge revelation where I want to go to Mexico and build houses for the poor, or take a job as a male stripper. But it is like there was this one new possibility. There is the possibility that somebody could want me.

That's all you get in terms of graphic details, because intimacy is, well, just that.

I reach over and touch her hair. It's wet. I trace the trail of moisture with my finger, right to the corner of her eye.

"You okay?"

She nods.

"Listen . . . "

"Shut up."

"I . . . "

"Angus, shut up."

Can't say I haven't heard that before. I wonder if she's mad at me, but when I put my arms around her, she backs into me, so if she is, she has a funny way of showing it.

At about three, I pop awake. *I didn't use a condom.* To a regular-sized guy, information like that causes debilitating panic. For a guy my size, it can turn cardio. What a jerk! I didn't even ask! All those times I watched that squiggly swimmer reach the egg first in sex ed, it never occurred to me it could be *my* squiggly swimmer. And there is *no* chance Sarah Byrnes is on birth control.

I start to wake her, but I can't. Unanticipated childbirth and matrimony aside, something in this feels so right, I refuse to mess it up. But either I don't sleep the rest of the night, or I dream I'm awake. Either way, I start the day *beat*.

Sarah jostles my shoulder. "Wake up."

"I'm awake."

"Let's do it."

I start to say we already did, but that's a really bad guy joke, plus I know she's talking about finding her mom.

"You sure?"

"I'm sure. Let's get it done before I'm not."

We both start to get out of bed, stop simultaneously when we realize there will be a plethora of nudity if we do. I'm at a way disadvantage. Sarah has a great body, all worked out and buff and everything. She worries about her *face*. I, on the other hand, look like fifty pounds of porridge in a twenty-five-pound bag. Man, I gotta get the swimming thing down.

"You first," we say together.

"No, *you* first." Two voices as one.

We dig around under the covers for our sweats. She giggles when she finds my underwear and tries them on. "Wow," she says. "Boxers or briefs? Tarp."

"She was at this breakfast place in the Sands," Sarah says. "It won't be easy if we find her; when she saw me last time she ran for it. God, I hated her that day. She was the only one who could save me, and she knew it. Shit! People thought my dad was so cool because he raised me alone. They had no idea what a beast he was."

"But he's in the slammer now," I say. "You don't

need her to do anything but talk. How could she at least not give you that?"

"Think what it would be like to face me if you were her. Forget what I want. How much would you hate yourself if you walked out and let your kid be raised by a monster? How could you look them in the eye?"

"I know. I couldn't. But wouldn't you want *some* shot at redemption?"

"You and I would, but you and I wouldn't have done what she did."

This conversation is *surreal*. I'm trying to imagine the unimaginable, which Sarah has lived. She's such a hero to me. If this were *my* mom, I'd be down here with a baseball bat.

"It was awful last time. I let everything ride on it. I sat in that car with Ms. Lemry on the way here and envisioned everything but what happened. It was five minutes from the time we saw her in the restaurant till it was over. I survived the next week only because of Moby and Lemry. There's no substitute for a family, but real friends can save you." She stops in the middle of the sidewalk and turns to me. "When you've wandered in the desert all your life, you'd be surprised what one sip of water can do."

I've been aware of people's subtle glances all this

time we've been walking. Sarah's scars aren't in a league with Elephant Man or that kid in *Mask*, but they're the first thing you notice. This is what it's like for her on any street in any town, all her life.

I would be tired.

"Sandy Byrnes? She worked here until about a month ago, but she left to go to California."

"Dang." I'm talking to Daytime Manager Bob Newman at the counter. As determined as Sarah is to go through with this, when we walked in she got short of breath and sat on the bench where others are waiting to be seated. "A month. Do you know where in California?"

"I believe it was Redding. Up north near Mount Shasta."

"You don't have an address or, like, a number? Maybe her cell?"

"I'm certain we have her numbers from when she was here, but I'm not at liberty to give them."

"We're relatives." Then I do what I do almost as well as I played football; I lie my ass off. "We came down to surprise Aunt Sandy. She hasn't seen us for almost ten years. We both graduated from high school this year and came down on vacation, you know, like, to surprise her.

She used to baby-sit for us." I point to Sarah. "That's my cousin. Her parents died in a car accident when she was little. She lived with us, but Sandy took care of us mostly."

Daytime Manager Bob Newman starts to soften.

"It was a train."

"What?"

"Her parents. They were killed at a railroad crossing. A train."

He glances at Sarah, who's still trying to get her breath. She looks plenty pathetic.

"Remains were unrecognizable," I say.

"You better be telling me the truth, young man."

"On my mother's grave, sir."

"Your mother's dead, too?"

"Oh, no, sir. I meant to say on *her* mother's grave." I nod toward Sarah.

Daytime Manager Bob Newman disappears for a moment, then returns. "Listen, son, Sandy left in pretty bad shape. I have no idea what it was all about, but we were all very worried. She worked here for years, and all of a sudden she was just panicked. If the two of you help her, more power to you. I've written her address on this slip of paper with the phone number she had all the time she worked here. Several of us have called; all we've gotten is the answering machine. I'd appreciate it if you said you got this address from a family member."

"Your wish is my command. We were never here. And don't worry, she'll be overwhelmed to see us." Overwhelmed is a word with a number of connotations. I should write political speeches.

"Slight right turn in one-point-one miles." I love my GPS lady. For most of my driving life, she has been my girlfriend. She doesn't get mad no matter how many times you cross her. The worst she ever says is, "At your earliest convenience, make a legal U-turn." That and "Please return to the highlighted route." Even if I'd had fifty girlfriends, I'm pretty sure Bathsheba would be the most forgiving one. I call her Bathsheba because in real life she gives me directions on the road; in my fantasy life she gives me directions in . . . never mind. That's over. I've got a girlfriend.

My girlfriend is pretty quiet right now as we head for the address I finessed from Daytime Manager Bob Newman.

"He said they were still getting the answering machine. You don't run off and leave your answering machine. Bet she's there. Keep driving?"

Sarah is crouched, her feet planted on the dashboard.

Mere mortals would lose a foot doing that in my car, but I barely notice. You don't pull protocol on your girlfriend when she's riding toward hell. And when she can arguably kick your ass. "Keep driving. I mean, what could she have to lose after we tell her my dad's put away for at least fifteen years? It's not like I want to live with her." She's talking herself into it.

"Exactly. And this can be the first step on her road to forgiveness."

Sarah shoots a look at me that, were it a snake, would be an Inland Taipan, which lives in Australia and can put out enough venom with one bite to kill a hundred people. *One* person dies mondo rapido. Even a fat guy.

"Well, maybe not forgiveness."

"Maybe not."

"Redemption, then. For her. Not you. Her."

"Just drive," Sarah says. Should this relationship flower, I can imagine there will be one or two difficult times.

"Destination on the left in point-five miles," Bathsheba says. Sarah takes a deep breath, scrunches farther into the seat.

I see the U-Haul truck first, parked at the edge of the first lawn in the Mountain Homes trailer park.

"You have arrived," Bathsheba says as I pull next to it.

"Wait here." I walk around to the back to see the truck half loaded. The front door is ajar, and I hear movement inside.

"She's in there," I tell Sarah when I get back in the car.

Sarah nods; stares.

"Wanna turn around and go?"

She shakes her head, her lips pursed.

We sit a moment, watching. I do *not* know what to do. When Sarah is this focused, you wait; and you build anxiety.

I can't take it. "You want me to stay in the car or go in?"

She looks over at me, then back at the giant U-Haul.

"At least we got here before she took off," I say.

"I wish I knew what I want out of this," she says finally.

"You're wrapping things up," I say. "Ending this part of your life and moving on. Closure, as they say."

"There's more than that."

"Say it."

"All my life, the one thing I've never been able

to let go of is 'what if.'" What if my dad hadn't come home that night? Or what if he'd just broken my arm or thrown me across the room? What if my mother had found a way to protect me, to get me away and run? The one thing everyone always said was that I was a beautiful kid. I changed my mother's life. She used to walk down the streets all haggard and depressed, wearing sunglasses on cloudy days or long sleeves on warm days to hide the bruises. Then I came along, and people who would never have noticed her, at least noticed *me*. And she felt like someone. I was pretty enough to get my mother noticed."

"You lost a lot."

Understated like a true dipshit.

"I've never been able to stop saying 'what if.' I think I want her to tell me there *is* no 'what if,' that there was no way she could have done anything different. Destiny. It *had* to happen."

"What would that do?"

"I could stop hoping," she says, and closes her eyes. "I could stop wishing."

This probably isn't the time for it, but I can't help myself. "Listen, Sarah. I don't know what last night was to you, or what this trip has been. But I'm in this. I mean, I thought I was never going to get the chance to sleep with . . . to have . . . to *make love*. I thought it would never happen. I've been a comedian and I've been in-your-face all my life, but I've never been boyfriend material. I'm fat, but more than that, I've always been scared. My parents, *all* of them, have been great when it comes to taking care of me and loving me and making me feel wanted, but there's enough neurosis among them to start a fucking clinic."

Sarah stares.

"Listen, I'll swim. I will. I always knew I'd have to do something after football to keep me from blowing up like the *Hindenburg*. Swimming could be it. It'll take some work. I've tried it; I'm no natural. But I'll do it. I'll pare down like your other fat friend."

Sarah puts her hand on my knee. "Angus," she says.

"Yeah?"

"Would you shut the fuck up?"

Another request I've heard before.

"I just need to get through this, okay? We'll talk about all that later. It was the first time for me, too. It was nice."

"I wanted you to know you can't lose *everything* if you don't want to," I say. "I will shut the fuck up now . . . but remember . . . "

"Angus."

"Shut the fuck up?"

Inside the single-wide, Sarah's mother looks up from the cardboard box into which she is cramming her Melmac dishes, and turns instantly pale.

Sarah says, "Hey."

Her mother sucks the air out of the room.

In the dead silence I step forward. "I'm Angus," I say, putting out my hand. "I'm Sarah's, uh . . . chauffeur."

She ignores my hand; or, more likely, doesn't see it. "What are you doing here? I thought—"

"You'd never see me again?" Sarah says. "I thought that, too. I came to tell you my dad's in jail. It'll be at least fifteen years before he's eligible for parole. You're safe. I thought I needed you to testify when I was here before, but it's over, that's all. I thought you should know."

Sarah's mom drops the plate she was holding into the box and sits back on the floor, speechless.

I was born Mr. Fix-It. I cannot reconcile the silent scream between them, but even *I'm* smart enough to keep my mouth shut.

"Is there a way," Sarah says, and hesitates, points to her face. "*Was* there a way for this not to have happened?

Was there *anything* in you that could have grabbed me and run? Or escaped before it even was possible?"

Sandy Byrnes rises, tears streaming down her face, closes the maybe ten feet between them, shaking her head with each step. She touches Sarah's face. "No," she says. "I was weak, nobody. I'm still nobody. Whatever awful thing he was going to do, he was going to do." She looks at her watch, then toward the front door. "I'm sorry," she says. "You can say whatever you want to say to me, or think whatever you want to think. It can't be half as bad as what I tell myself every day."

Sarah nods. Her shoulders slump. I can't tell if she's defeated or relieved. Then, "If it helps," she says, "some people stepped up to help."

Her mother breaks into sobs, nodding. "It helps."

"And because of them, I won't be nobody. I won't be like you. I'll try to stop hating you, I will. I'll try to forgive you. But I can't say that will happen."

Her mother continues nodding, bent over. Tears fall directly to the floor. "You have to go now," she says. "You've seen all there is of me." She straightens up, takes a deep breath, glances at her watch again, then nervously toward the door. "Please. Go."

"Is that the last word you want me to hear?" Sarah says. Ice forms in her voice.

Sandy starts to respond, glances at the door again, and simply nods.

I rise and put my hand in the middle of Sarah's back. "Let's blow this pop stand, baby," I whisper. "You got all you're going to get." In my heart of hearts, I want to beat Sarah Byrnes's mother to death. In the furthest corners of my imagination I cannot accommodate *anyone* having done what she did, lived all those years with it, then simply saying, "Go."

We stand on the stoop outside the trailer, catching our breath. A girl, maybe junior high, peddles her bike up the street. A dog barks. The wind rustles a broad-leafed tree. We walk toward the car; Sandy Byrnes stands in her doorway, looks down the street, and I see a flash of panic. She glances back at us. "You need to go," she says. "Hurry."

Something is not right here. Hell, there's a lot not right, but something specific. I see the girl on the bike approaching. She looks right at us, peddling faster. Sarah's mom looks directly at her, turns away. *That's* where the panic is coming from.

"We'll go in a minute," I say, and squat.

Sandy disappears into the trailer.

Sarah says, "Let's go now, Angus. I know what I need to know."

"In a sec," I say, and stay put.

Sarah walks to the car. The girl rides past her, and their eyes lock. The girl slows. Sarah turns. The girl drops her bike in the yard, glances back at Sarah, says hi to me, and yells, "Mom!" She disappears into the trailer.

Sarah freezes, staring at the bike lying on the lawn. I run to her, trace her gaze to the bike. Attached to the middle of the handlebars by two thin wires, a personalized license plate—the kind you get in any drugstore in the country—reads SARAH.

"Let's go," I say.

Sarah stalks toward the trailer.

"Come on, Sarah. Let's go."

She disappears through the door. *Shit.*

Might as well make it a party. When I get to the door, Sarah is face-to-face with her sister. Backlit by the living-room window, their profiles are astonishingly similar. My Sarah is bigger and stronger, but Little Sarah is a miniature replica. Their mother sits on the couch.

Little Sarah says, "Hi. Who are you?"

"I'm Sarah."

"Really? Me, too. What are you doing here? Do you know my mother?"

"Not really," Sarah says. "I knew her a long time ago." She reaches up, almost involuntarily, and runs the back of her finger along Little Sarah's face. Little Sarah doesn't pull back, stares at Sarah's scars.

"What happened?"

"A guy burned me," Sarah says, and turns toward the door. "Get me out of here," she whispers, and steps past me.

In less than a minute we're speeding toward the freeway.

"She replaced me."

I start to protest, reframe it, but no. She replaced her. We've driven in silence more than an hour; leaving the outskirts of Reno, then Sparks, in the rearview mirror, hurtling into the desert. I'm averaging twenty miles above the speed limit, trying to get the girl I hope to love far away from that horror as fast as I can. Man, nobody should have to go through that. That shit is biblical.

We ride another half hour or so, then, "Right when you think things can't get worse."

"It gets *way* worse," I say back.

I want to say, It's okay. Screw her. You don't need her. But it's her *mom*. I mean, she marries a guy mean enough to scar you for life, then he does, then she *leaves*, for Christ sake. She *leaves*. How do you not take your kid with? I can't stop asking that question. I mean, you buy your kid a dog, the dog gets rabies, and you send them out to play? It isn't okay; it will never be okay, so I don't say, "It's okay."

"She was pregnant. She left because she was pregnant," Sarah says. "That girl was just the right age. I was already ruined, and she knew she couldn't protect her new baby." She shakes her head, stares out at the desert whizzing by. "But she named her Sarah."

"I don't know what to say," I tell her. "That's just so goddam low."

She plugs in the Nano, and John Dawson Read sings sweet through the car speakers. "A friend of mine is going blind . . . "

"When I was little," Sarah says after long miles of the same song over and over, "I couldn't shake the idea that something was wrong with me. I mean, I knew I was burned, I knew *that* was wrong, but I couldn't shake that something was wrong with me before that. I thought I *must* have been shiny before it happened, because everyone *said* so. But it couldn't have been true, because every shiny thing I ever had, I protected; little charms and rings you got out of Cracker Jack, steely marbles, cheap necklaces. If it was shiny, I sheltered it. Even if my mother didn't take care of me, *I* would have found a way to protect me if I was really shiny. That's what I thought." She shakes her head, and for the first time in our short life together, I watch her floodgates give.

I pull the car onto the shoulder, shove it in park, and wrap my big ol' meaty arms around her. She struggles for a split second and melts, sobbing until the front of my shirt feels like my undershirt at the end of two-a-days in August.

"You're *way* shiny," I tell her. "You are."

She shakes her head no and sobs harder. I stroke her hair and rub her back and we sit.

I awake to a sharp *rap,* and my driver's side window is filled with the torso of a Nevada highway patrolman. "Everything all right in there?" he says as I roll down the window.

"Yes, sir."

"So why are you parked on the freeway and not at the rest stop two miles down the road?"

"It was kind of an emergency," I say. Sarah sits up, her scarred face streaked, hair matted.

"I was told on my radio this car's been here more than two hours."

"Yes, sir."

He bends down, peers in. Sarah glances at him, then away. But he sees her and must think he's looking at some of the most seriously pathetic shit he's seen all day. He nods. "This is unusual enough for probable cause," he says. "I could search your car."

"For what?"

"Drugs, whatever."

"Man, if you search this car and find some drugs, I'll split them with you sixty-forty. If there were drugs in this car, I can assure you you'd have to do stomach surgery to find them. This has been one perfectly shitty day."

I guess the truth has a ring of truth to it, because instead of making me pop the trunk, he says, "Well, maybe tomorrow will be a better one. You can make mine better by moving down to the rest stop."

In Winnemucca, we stop for food. Neither of us is hungry, but we've been in this car long enough that if I don't get out my fat ass will melt into the upholstery. Plus, the last thing in the world I have to be is hungry, to want to eat. Sarah orders orange juice and coffee and an English muffin. I'm tempted to get the Infinite Burger. The menu says if you eat it all, it's free; if not, you pay double. I usually warm up to that kind of challenge real quick, but it would not be impressive in the way

I currently want to be impressive. "I'll take the club sandwich," I tell the waiter.

"Good choice," she says.

"And I'd like the club tenderized."

That gets a little smile out of Sarah, though the waitress looks at me like I'm out of my big fat mind. Guess they don't do puns in Winnemucca.

"What in the world am I gonna do now?" Sarah says as the waitress leaves to put in our order.

"Probably best to sit with it awhile," I say. "Sometimes if you do that, an answer comes that you wouldn't expect.

She slouches. "Maybe. I don't guess I have a choice. It's not like I have a plan."

"I've got a plan," I tell her. "Maybe not a plan; maybe an idea."

She shrugs. "Let's hear it."

"You ever had a boyfriend?"

"Do I look like I've ever had a boyfriend? Jesus, Angus."

"Well, I've never had a girlfriend, so I'm seeing a starting place."

"A starting place." Man, Sarah can be major-league sarcastic when she wants to be. If I were the kind of guy to get intimidated, that might do it. Come to think of it, I am the kind of guy to get intimidated. But I have a history of overcoming that.

"Why don't we be in love?"

"Why don't we be in love?" Again, it sounded better when I said it. "How do you just be in love?"

"You just do it, I think. You hold hands and tell each other shit you don't tell anyone else. You go cool places. You do . . . what we did last night."

The waitress delivers our food just in time to hear, "What we did last night." Sarah blushes and looks down, but the waitress doesn't skip a beat. I bet what we did last night gets done a lot in Winnemucca. Unless you're a card shark, it doesn't look like there's a lot else to do.

Sarah eats quietly while I look between bread slices to see why they call it a club sandwich. "What do you have to lose?"

Her head snaps up. Fire burns in her eyes. "I have everything to lose, Angus Bethune. Everything. You want to know how I've stayed alive so far? By never wanting *any*thing. I've never asked for a Christmas present or a birthday present or even dessert. I take what is given to me. When you don't have anything, you can't lose anything. Shit, I'm scared to death 'cause Ms. Lemry and her husband want to adopt me. I'm eighteen. Legally it doesn't even mean anything and I'm still afraid of it. My other fat friend, Moby? He's going off to school on the coast. You know what happens to people who go their separate ways? They go their separate ways. I'm terrified he'll just sink into time. He's not even gone and I've told myself he is. What do I have to lose? Shit, Angus."

"Listen . . . "

"No, you listen. I held on to my mother my whole life. I dreamed that she was scheming to come get me. I have every one of those postcards she sent from Reno. She didn't sign them, didn't write on them. But I looked at those casinos and called them castles. They quit coming, and I stared at the old ones until I wore them out. Shit, somewhere back there that bitch of a mother of mine must have at least *thought* about coming for me. Then Ms. Lemry and I found her, and she was weak and scared. I got it in my head that I didn't really want her; not the real her, anyway. I had only wanted the idea of her.

"But when you said let's go find her, I realized it wasn't over. What if she didn't come back because she was scared of my dad? I thought. What if I could have her after all? And we go and she not only doesn't want me, she's *replaced* me."

"I know. We shouldn't have gone. It was a bad idea."

"Hell if it was," she says. "It was a fucking great

idea. This is how you find out what's *real*, Angus. You look it in the eye."

"Okay," I say, "it's real. That doesn't tell me why we can't be in love."

"Because right now you feel sorry for me. You like to help people, and you just watched me take one in the gut. But you know what? You're forgetting that I'm ugly. And six months from now, I'll still be ugly, and a year after that and a year after that. And you won't feel sorry for me anymore, and you'll notice like crazy. And I'll be stuck losing something I can't afford to lose."

Man, I hate it when somebody thinks they know what I'm thinking. Even if they do. "You're not ugly to me."

"Bullshit."

"Bullshit back. You're not. Hell, with my glasses off I can barely see you. And even if you were ugly, you're no uglier than me. You ever see those aliens on *Star Wars* or *Star Trek*? Dog noses, cookie-cutter fork things all down their cheeks, some of 'em. Pointy ears. How do you think they keep their generations going? I look at 'em and say, 'Hey, Movie Genius, what were you thinking when you created *that*?' But to them, they're not ugly, they just look like each other. If the world was made up of mostly fat people and burned people, we'd be fuckin' magazine models. And if that's true, then we are."

"Those aren't real things, Angus. They're either digital or created in a makeup place."

"Maybe, but you get the point." I reach across the table and grab her hand, and only get a little bit of mayonnaise on it. "This last year one of the studs on the football team paid a bunch of guys to vote for me to be our high school Winter Ball king. It must have cost him a fortune, but he's a rich kid. His girlfriend was the Winter Ball queen, and he had some sick shit going on where he wanted to teach us both a lesson. I'd messed him up pretty good on the football field, and who knows what he thought she did. Anyway, I'd been in love with this girl, like, forever, so even though I was embarrassed out of my mind, I wanted to go through with it, just so I could have my *moment* with her. You know, something to hold on to. Something to remember. She wasn't my *date*; she was showing up with him. I just had that one dance; that one little five-minute . . . *thing*."

Sarah nods. She does know that.

"So he gets drunk at the dance and embarrasses me and her, and she gets majorly pissed and leaves the dance with me. My five-minute thing turns into maybe an hour-and-a-half thing, because I get to buy her a milkshake and drive her home and sit in the car and talk for a little while. When it's done, I got way more than I expected. I got extra time and the satisfaction of knowing she dropped him like a molten turd. Then she went and got with some other asshole."

Sarah softens a little. "Welcome to Planet Earth, huh?"

"Yeah. It was over and I had the memory, the thing I was after in the first place. But you know what? Fuck that. There's no difference between a five-minute memory and an hour-and-a-half memory. I'm tired of living for memories. They're great, but they don't sustain you. They fade. They aren't shiny."

She looks away at my use of her word.

"It's the perfect word, Sarah Byrnes. You're shiny to me."

"I won't stay that way."

"Do you know a guy named Kyle Maynard?"

"No. Is Kyle Maynard shiny?" She can bounce back to sarcastic like a Super Ball.

"Fuckin' A, he's shiny. Kid was a high-school wrestler in Georgia. Went on to wrestle in college. Wanna know what's shiny about Kyle Maynard?"

"Lay it on me."

"Kyle Maynard was born with no arms below the elbow and no legs below the knee. He lost the first bazillion of his wrestling matches, but by the time he was a senior in high school, he was headed for state. You have any idea what his parents thought when they first saw him? No warning anywhere in the pregnancy, then *BAM!* We get a torso."

That gets her attention. Kyle Maynard gets everyone's attention.

"I don't know what his parents were thinking—like, how they did it—but they must have just told him to do things as if everyone had no arms and legs. He types fifty words a minute with no prosthetics. He has better handwriting than I have. Only it ain't handwriting, it's stub writing. The guy just acts like the rest of the world's like him."

Sarah looks down at her body. "Well," she says, "I'm not like Kyle Maynard. I have arms and legs."

"Yeah, but here's the deal. I didn't expect to tell you a story about Kyle Maynard and have you forget that your dumb bitch mother left you in the eye of some awful hurricane and then replaced you. The deal is, if everyone had scars on their faces, then we'd add that into pretty. I'm telling you, Sarah Byrnes, I can add that into pretty. I already have. I can't fuckin' see anyway, and what happened last night is just *in* me. I don't want to ever have to give it up. The difference between you and Kyle Maynard is, he came into the world with his condition and was loved. You came in without yours, but contempt and . . . indifference, I guess . . . gave it to you. And you weren't loved. I can't go back into your childhood and love you. If I could, I would. I swear to God I would. But I can love you now. And I do."

She is quiet a long time, then finally, "I don't know if I can do this, Angus. I feel like I was loved by Moby, my other fat guy, but not in, you know, *that* way. There was a time, when he fell in love with this really cool girl, that I thought I wouldn't survive. I mean, I thought I'd kill myself. I had the plan. It scared me so much I took it away from myself, even the possibility. If I stopped wanting, no one could hurt me. I don't know."

I'm desperate. "Look, I know nobody can promise anything forever. Shit, my parents promised to love, honor, and whatever when they first got married, and they turned out not to even want the same *gender*. But I can promise I'll always tell you the truth. I can promise you no surprises. Hey, I don't like the way people look at me either."

"Yeah, but your 'condition' is fixable. Like Moby's."

"Yeah, but I'm not going to fix it. If you'd seen me in the pool the other day, you'd believe me."

She grimaces.

"I'm a *way* bigger dickwad than you are. You'll get tired of me a long time before I could get tired of you."

I'm a hell of a debater. I may or may not be smart, but I'll wear you down.

A fiery sunset explodes on the western horizon as we drive up out of Winnemucca toward home. Maybe fifty miles up the road, Sarah scoots over toward me and lays her hand in my lap. We ride another twenty or thirty miles like that, her hand in my lap and mine over hers.

"We're not even going to the same college," she says. "What about that?"

"We change our plans. I'll go where you go."

"It's too late to change."

"Then I'll work in McDonald's for a semester and bulk up. Don't even think about trying to change my mind."

Our dilemma is resolved. It's nearing the middle of August. I contacted the University of Idaho and told them the next nuclear scientist to come out of there would have to be someone other than me; I'd been made a better offer by Burger King. My new idea will depend on Sarah Byrnes's willingness to do the same.

"You've curbed global warming?" she says.

"Close. Look at this." I hand her two brochures.

"Rather than make me read them, why don't you just tell me, like you'll do anyway."

"As you wish," I say with a flair. "It's a place called Mountain Lightning, up out of Bozeman, Montana, way high in the Rockies."

"Mountain Lightning."

I ignore her dismissiveness. You have to do that if you're going to love Sarah Byrnes. She can flat cut you up with a look, or a comment. "It's like a camp."

"Oh, I *love* to camp. Nothing like lying on the hard ground and peeing in a hole and freezing your butt off under a beautiful but arctic sky high in the Rocky fucking Mountains."

"Yeah, there probably is nothing like that, but this is a camp with cabins and beds and all the amenities. Well, not satellite TV, but no hard ground to sleep on either. Look. It's for *blind* kids. It says here their philosophy is kind of like what I thought Kyle Maynard's parents' philosophy was. Just pretend everyone's like you. They have sighted counselors and blind counselors. Without my glasses, I almost cross over. I'm, like, *bilingual* in their world. And look here. They want counselors with 'expressive' language skills, 'people good at describing the physical world with passion.' There's formal writing and informal conversations and all kinds of other stuff. It says right here, 'There has never been a good employee of Mountain Lightning who didn't get at least as much as he or she gave.'"

Sarah takes the brochures out of my hand. "Wonder what they mean by that?"

"Probably that they don't pay much. But we go where nobody sees us before they know us. It's a year-round residential outfit. This is the perfect time to apply because a lot of the summer employees go back to school now."

"I don't know, Angus."

I sing: "A friend of mine is going blind but through the dimness, he sees so much better than me." I sing it badly. "We'll be in the dimness, Sarah. *Pleeeze!* We can go to college any time. I mean, we know we will. But this is a once in a lifetime. It's beautiful, I mean, look at these pictures." I hold open the brochure. "Pleeeze, Sarah, think about it." I stop and smile. "See, I told you, you'd get tired of me long before the other way around."

She takes the brochures. "I'll think about it."

■ ■ ■

Dinner's over. The mess hall is clean; dishes washed, tables scrubbed. Sarah and I sit on the porch outside the main meeting hall, waiting to tutor some of the older kids with their homework. It's a smaller group in the fall. Many of the summer campers have gone to their homes and back to school. The fall and winter kids are a little more troubled overall; some of them have no place but here. Sarah and I are here as aides. Room and board and seventy-five dollars a week. In my first days I felt anxiety retreat on a daily basis. Nobody looked at me with disapproval as I lumbered over the trails or talked a group through the intricate paths from the cabins to the meeting hall or the school. The considerations I make to accommodate my charges' lack of sight are nothing compared to the relief of living with people who don't judge me before they know me.

Sarah is a different person. She works with younger kids than I do, but she is *so* much better at it than I am. Such a natural. It makes me wonder what she would be by now if she hadn't spent her life flying under her father's radar and dodging the slings and arrows of her peers. A monstrous weight has been lifted.

"Tell me this wasn't a good idea," I say now, leaning

back on the steps and staring at the moon rising through the trees, nearly full.

"It was a good idea, Angus. I'm sorry I doubted you." She laughs. "I'll never doubt you again, Angus." Clearly she's retained her command of the facetious uppercut. Sarah Byrnes will doubt me on a regular basis.

"I guess you won't," I say anyway.

A little girl whose name I don't know walks onto the porch. She's maybe six or seven.

"Hey, Amanda," Sarah says.

"Hey, Sarah."

"Wanna come sit with us?"

"Uh-huh."

She feels her way toward us, sits on the far side of Sarah from me.

"This is Angus."

Amanda says, "Hi, Angus."

I say hi back.

"Angus works with the bigger kids."

"Can he see?"

"He can see, but he has everything else wrong with him."

Amanda turns toward me. "What all's wrong with you, Angus?"

"I snore. I drool. I eat children."

"Huh-*uh*!"

"Sometimes I don't go to the bathroom for a month."

Amanda giggles, turns to Sarah. "They said the moon was big tonight."

"Very big," she says. "Almost a full moon."

"What does it look like?"

"Well, it's round, and very bright. It seems warm. If we were closer, it would be much bigger, but from here it's about this big—can I show you with your hands?"

"Yes."

"Point your fingers."

Amanda extends her fingers. Sarah takes her forearms, points those fingers toward the moon, and draws a perfect circle around it. "It has lots of bumps and lines where the ground is uneven. You know, mountains and valleys and things like that. Like the ground here, only without bushes or trees." Sarah looks at me and smiles. "It's shiny," she says.

Amanda nods.

We sit on the porch awhile. Amanda leans into the crook of Sarah's arm. After a bit, she says, "Sarah?"

"Yeah?

"Can I touch your face? I forget what you look like."

"Of course," Sarah says, and turns toward her. Sarah Byrnes is so fucking brave.

Amanda touches her softly, traces her tiny fingers along Sarah's scars, cups Sarah's chin in her palms. She feels around Sarah's eyes, and Sarah closes them and smiles. Amanda touches her smile and traces her lips. She withdraws her hands and giggles slightly.

"What?" Sarah giggles back.

"Sarah Byrnes has a face like the moon."

Nak's Notes
First Impressions
Transcribed directly from digital recorder

NAME: *Montana West (no fooling)*

AGE: *17*

REASONS TO BE PISSED: *Daddy's chairman of the school board;
that there by itself would piss most kids off. Adopted; early childhood abandonment. Locked in a power struggle with her daddy,
who don't leave her much wiggle room. Passive momma. (That's
a bad combo.)*

SIGNIFICANT CHARACTERISTICS: *Real perty; don't know what
to do with it. Personal exterior decoration. Writes real good.
Maybe a little identity trouble.*

COPING SKILLS: *Does that thing they call goth—all kinds of
metal in her—famous tattoo, likes to use the school newspaper
like a weapon. Another smart one. Kinda in your face.*

PROGNOSIS: *Look the hell out. She's gonna be just fine.*

NAME: *Trey Chase*

AGE: *17*

REASONS TO BE PISSED: *Not a lot. This boy don't seem to let a lot get under his skin. Lost his parents.*

SIGNIFICANT CHARACTERISTICS: *Dead-on handsome, got that bad-boy thing going. Good athlete. Might be smart but ain't gonna let you see it.*

COPING SKILLS: *Seems to soothe his savage self with the company of the ladies, sits back and checks things out, doesn't show his hand real quick.*

PROGNOSIS: *This boy could be president.*

Montana Wild

"Montana, we're going to have to change the lead story."

"Change it how?"

"Dump it. We ran up against the censors. Again." Dr. Conroy shakes her head. "We didn't have much of a chance with this one."

"How does it get censored? It's a story about medical marijuana, for crying out loud. It's, like, about cancer and terminal illness. I put a lot of work into that."

"Mr. Remington and Dr. Holden both say the whole thing is a ruse to legalize marijuana, make it so anyone can get their hands on it."

"So because that's what they *think*, I have to report it that way. What do *you* think?"

"You know what I think about censorship," Dr. Conroy says. "But I don't have the power to change their minds."

"Which means you're not a concrete worker. Did you show them the article? There isn't one thing in there about recreational use."

"Of course I showed them the article."

"And . . . "

"And I doubt either one of them read it. In fact I'll bet Remington is as far as it got."

"That's not fair."

"It's as fair as it would be if he showed it to Dr. Holden. Mr. Remington is a Kennedy compared to Dr. Holden."

"So I wrote it for nothing," Montana says.

"You wrote it for an A," Dr. Conroy says back. "Just because we can't publish it doesn't mean you don't get a grade. Look, in another year, you'll be in college. Your university newspaper would print this in a minute. You make your point; you have great quotes. It's succinct. A work."

Montana stares at the article. "I didn't write it for a grade. I can get an A anytime. I wrote it to publish."

"I know, Montana. But you had to realize there wasn't a great chance. I mean, how many of your articles have those guys stopped? You did hunting, which you called 'slaughtering animals for fun'; you did scientific experimentation on animals, which you called the same thing. You did an article comparing Christianity with Greek mythology. What else?"

"Gay marriage."

"Uh-huh."

"Isn't there a way around this?"

Dr. Conroy smiles. "We can take any one of those articles all the way to the school board."

"Right," Montana says. "To my dad. *He* makes *Holden* look like a Kennedy."

"Lessons in relativity, huh?" Dr. Conroy says.

"What do you mean?"

"You know, 'How far right do you have to go to make *blank* look like a Kennedy?' I'll bet it's close to infinite."

"Huh. If you get much further right than my dad, you're in outer space."

"He means well, Montana."

"He means ill."

"I believe your father thinks he's keeping people . . . *children* . . . safe when he makes those decisions."

Montana lays her books on Dr. Conroy's desk and hoists herself up. "How did this happen?"

Dr. Conroy says, "How did what happen?"

"I'm young and supposedly optimistic. You're old and supposedly cynical from experience. How come I get it that my dad is intentionally a dick and you cling to a possibility that isn't possible?"

"That bad, huh?"

"I'm just glad I'm adopted," Montana says. "At least I don't have to worry about his DNA getting on me."

Dr. Conroy loves the way Montana sees and says things, though political correctness doesn't always allow her to say so. She'd give a chunk of her paycheck to have more writers like her.

"God is a wonderful entity," Montana says. "Takes one look at my father, recognizes the cosmic mistake, and gives him zero sperm count."

Dr. Conroy laughs out loud. "How in the world would you know that?"

"I heard them fighting. That's a real weapon, I think; sperm count. When she said it, he shut *up*."

"Well, it's an adult weapon. You need a license to use it."

"Yeah, I know. I took it for a trial run."

"Grounded?"

"Till I'm thirty."

Dr. Conroy stares at the medical marijuana article.

"I'd have a backup to this if you want to keep your name above the fold."

Montana twirls her cheek stud between thumb and forefinger. "Hmm."

"Pick your battles, darlin'."

"Maybe I'll do that feature on how cheerleaders get such muscular calves."

"The PE department would love it."

"Yeah, I could get back in their good graces for my 'Why I Need PE to Get into Bryn Mawr' article."

"If I remember correctly, the entire text of that article was 'NOT.'"

Montana waves without looking back as she exits.

Interesting kid, Dr. Conroy thinks as the door closes in slow motion against the hydraulic arm. Two years ago, as a sophomore, Montana was a beauty queen. Long dark hair, killer brown eyes, the lean, muscular body of a dancer. Dated the senior tight end on the football team. Came back this year with piercings where most girls don't know they have places, the famous worm tattoo, and an attitude toward authority that made her new dark appearance look like child's play. I guess they have to find their places to stand.

■　■　■

Montana opens the front door to see her sister facing the corner opposite the front door. "Hey, little sis, what'd you do this time?"

"Nothin'."

"Put you in the corner for nothin', huh. Better not ever *do* anything or they'll skin you alive. Where's Mom?"

"I don't care."

"Maybe I can negotiate your release."

"In the kitchen. Making poison."

"I'll put food coloring in it," Montana says. "So we can trace which food she puts it in."

The kitchen door swings closed behind her. "Hey, Mom."

Her mother is stirring a pot, doesn't turn around. "Hi."

"How long is the rat in the corner for?"

"Until she can tell me why I put her there in the first place."

How familiar is *that*? "Mom, do you know what kids like her think about in the corner?"

"What."

"We think about outlasting you. And how we're gonna get even."

"We?"

Montana rolls her eyes. "Mom, I smeared poop in the dryer, turned it on high, and hid in the closet. I'm one of those kids."

"You *were* one of those kids."

"We'll see," Montana says. "Now how does Tara get out of the corner?"

"She tells me what got her in there."

"Which was . . . "

"Ask her. Montana, don't get too used to her. I don't know that we can keep her. Nothing seems to work. I've tried every kind of star chart and sticker chart her therapist or I can think of, and she just gets worse. I'm at wit's end."

"Come on, Mom. I smeared shit inside the *dryer* and you didn't get rid of me."

"We call that poop around here, young lady, and I was younger then. I thought there was a chance for you. This little girl turns everything sour. Everything."

Montana walks back into the living room.

"Hey, little girl."

"I hate her."

"Yeah," Montana says.

"They're gonna give me away."

"Naw, nobody else wants you." There's a moment of silence, and Montana sees Tara's shoulders slump.

"'Cept me," she says. "Let's get you out of this corner. What did you do to get in here?"

"Nothin'."

"Did that nothin' have to do with poop?"

"Prob'ly."

"Did it have to do with poop that didn't go into the toilet?"

"Prob'ly."

"Is it somewhere in your room?"

"Prob'ly."

"Where Mom can't find it, even if she can smell it?"

"Prob'ly."

"Let's go get it. Let's find the poop and put it where it belongs and set you free."

Tara is quiet.

"Little sis, what are you doing? Mom's not kidding when she says you can't stay if you keep doing that. And you don't *wanna* see Dad get all crazy like he does."

"I know."

"Stay here a minute."

Back in the kitchen she says, "Tara and I are going on a scavenger hunt, okay?"

"Tara's in the corner."

"Well, I'm taking her *out* of the corner so she can go find what you put her in the corner for and put it in the toilet. Then she'll come in and tell you why she was in the corner."

They go into Tara's bedroom, where Tara sits on the bed, staring at the door.

"Jeez. What did you eat? Show me where it is."

Tara sets her jaw.

"Don't mess with me, little sis. That might work with Mom, but you know it gets no play with me."

"Under the bed," Tara says.

"Gawd. This place smells like an outhouse."

"What's that?"

"A place that smells bad." Montana is on her hands and knees, looking under the bed for the offending excrement. "I don't see it."

"It's kinda rubbed."

Montana furrows her brow. Tara joins her on her hands and knees.

"Kinda rubbed? This carries the hint of premeditation."

Tara stares questioningly.

"It means you did it on purpose. You thought about it before you did it."

"Huh-uh."

"Uh-huh."

"Are they gonna gimme away?"

"I don't know," Montana says. "Why do you care? I mean, you always pick the thing that makes them the maddest. It's like you *want* to be given away."

"*You* pick the thing that makes Daddy West the maddest."

"Everything makes Daddy West the maddest. And that's different. I've been here long enough I can be a bitch. You can't start out like that." Montana swallows her lie. This kid could *be* her, back before her adoption when she came into foster care. Seven placements in three months. It wasn't a record, but it would do until she found what the record was. Hell on wheels at four years old. Ached for a mother she can barely remember now, and for whom she still aches. Tara is six, but that's about the only difference.

"Why do you keep hiding your poop, little sis? How are you going to make Momma want to keep you? You have to make them think they're doing something good for you. Do you *want* her to give you up?"

"I hate methamphetamine," Tara says. She pronounces it perfectly.

"That's a good thing to hate," Montana says back. "I hate methamphetamine, too."

"If I could throw methamphetamine in the ocean, I could get my real mom back."

"You sure could," Montana says. "But the only person who can throw methamphetamine in the ocean is your mom. So far she's not doing so hot, and until she drowns it, you've got to be good so you can stay here, and that means you have to stop hiding your poop."

"I get so *mad*. And my poop is mad, too. If it could talk it would say, 'I'M SO MAD!' I poop 'cause I'm mad I can't live with my mom. It wasn't her fault, it was Greg's. He was always asleep when he was s'posed to take care of me when my mom was usin' meth. My mom's not gonna do what she's s'posed to do to get me back. I'm really scared she doesn't *want* me back. That's the worst thing."

"Yup. When you and your poop get so mad, you gotta hide it in the toilet. It's not Mommy West that's making you mad."

"It's CPS."

"Yeah, but we've talked about this. CPS doesn't make your mom use meth. Your *mom* makes your mom use meth."

"If I was there I bet I could make her stop."

"Bet you couldn't. You could make her not use it in front of you, but you know meth."

"Yeah, but if I could be there I could trick the CPS lady again. I could make it look like Mom's not usin' it.

I did it before. Besides, sometimes CPS makes her feel bad and that's when she uses it. You use meth when you feel bad."

"Other way around, little sis. You use meth and you can't get your kid back and then you feel bad. Your mom's making a big mistake giving you up to Mommy West. But if you don't be good, which means quit hiding your poop and sneaking around at night trying to find things out, Mommy and Daddy West will give you up too. Listen, you're mad 'cause you're scared. I was just like you. If you talk about being scared, you might not have to poop. Get mad. Yell and scream. You don't see me pooping when I get mad."

Tara grimaces. There's no answer.

"So can you do it? Do you know how bad I'm going to feel if they give you up?"

"I don't want to go away from you. I'll try to use words to get it out instead of poop it out."

"That's my girl. You have to remember, if you don't want to give *me* up, you can't do things that will make Mommy West give *you* up. If you can't have your mom, *while* you can't have your mom, you want Mommy West, right?

"I WANT HER TO MAKE ME FEEL BAD!"

Montana grabs Tara and holds her tight. Tara

squirms a moment, then surrenders. How do you tell somebody that? How can she tell her mother that feeling bad feels *right* when everything in your world is wrong; that at first you need your foster parents to make things *familiar,* which in this case means fucked up. It makes such sense at a heart level, but even for a wordsmith like Montana West, it's impossible to articulate. It's *so* true, and it sounds *so* crazy.

"We're going to get a hot wet rag and some cleaner," Montana says, "and I'm going to lift up the bed and you're going to scrub the poop off and then you're going to go tell Mom what you did to get in the corner, which is you crapped in a no-crapping zone. Got it?"

The third period bell rings, and Montana hangs back. "I'm thinking of dropping this class," she says.

"Look over there at the door," Dr. Conroy says, and Montana does.

"At that area on the floor right in front of the door."

Montana does that, too.

"Now picture my dead body lying there," Dr. Conroy says, "because you will have to step over it if you try to drop this class."

"I can't write any of the stuff I want to write."

"Well, then write the hell out of something you *don't* want to write."

"Like what?"

"You can't think of anything you don't want to write? How about the football playoffs?"

Montana looks at Dr. Conroy like she just dropped a dead fish into her latte.

"Looks like we've found it," Dr. Conroy says. "The football playoffs."

"Ronnie Jackson does sports," Montana says. "What are you going to do, kick him over to fashion?"

"We don't have fashion."

"But you get the point."

"No, I'm not taking Ronnie off sports," Dr. Conroy says, "but you can do a human interest piece. Profile a player who doesn't usually get a lot of attention, or write about some other aspect of the sport."

Montana stares at the ceiling. "This *so* sucks."

"Listen," Dr. Conroy says. "I know passing everything through the principal's office doesn't reflect what the real world's going to be like. But truth is, when you get to college, or if you join a major newspaper, they're going to give you assignments that would make a football playoff piece look Pulitzer-worthy. They start everyone at the bottom. So instead of considering yourself the crack columnist of your high-school newspaper, consider yourself at the lowest level of the next step up. It'll keep you ahead of the game."

Montana walks away shaking her head. "Football playoffs."

"This is a personality profile? What's that?"

"It's where I profile your personality." Montana says.

"That definition would get you a C- in English," Trey Chase says.

"I didn't know football players took English."

Trey smiles, and Montana almost melts. She understands where this guy gets his rep. "I'm just looking for a different angle on the football team," she says.

"Coach told me to be careful," Trey says. "He says you're a muckraker."

"Only when there's muck to rake," she says back. "Shall we get on with this?"

"Sure."

"Mind if I record it?"

"Yup."

"You do mind?"

"I do mind," Trey says. "I only let people record me making late night 1-900 calls."

Montana shakes her head, hits the record button on her digital recorder, and sets it on the table between them, closer to Trey than to her to accommodate the cafeteria background noise.

"So what made you turn out for football in the first place?"

Trey smiles and stares at the recorder.

"You were serious."

"Serious as AIDS," he says as she reaches over and hits the stop button, then returns the recorder to her backpack. "A real journalist uses pen and paper anyway."

"Jeez." She drags out her notebook, closes her eyes a moment, and shakes her head.

"Wondering why you took this assignment?" Trey says.

"We'll see. What made you turn out for football in the first place?"

"Keep myself out of juvy."

"Really."

"Yup," Trey says. "Judge told my grandma if I'd turn out for football he'd hold off giving me a sentence. If I stayed with it a year, he'd drop the charges."

"You stayed with it four."

"I did. Actually I was going to take the sentence, but

my grandma slapped me so hard on the side of the head when I said it, I thought I heard church bells. Judge liked that. He smiled and said, 'You sure?'"

"What did you do to be standing before a judge in the first place?"

Trey smiles. "Let's just say I was in possession of some things I couldn't prove were mine."

"Like?"

"Things I couldn't prove were mine."

Montana nods and jots that down. Actually this could be fun; he makes her a bit uncomfortable. Bad boys. Watch out for bad boys. "So I know all the ESPN answers, and I'm looking for a different article than that; you know, in depth."

Trey smiles again, and Montana shifts in her seat. "In depth is usually a quarterback's interview," he says. "But let's give 'er a shot."

"How do you feel about the fact that football players are generally treated like gods in this school, that they get away with things the general population doesn't?"

"I like it."

"Excuse me?"

"I'm a football player. I like it."

That's the problem with asking a question you don't think you'll get an answer to. Dr. Conroy has warned her students about that. "So you agree? Football players get special privileges?"

Trey feigns confusion. "Oh, I thought you were telling me about some new policy."

"No, I was stating the obvious and asking what you think about it."

"Isn't that like, a trick question?"

"No, it's not a trick question—"

"I mean, if you say something you think is 'obviously true,' but it's not obviously true to me, doesn't that give you an advantage, like to get my ass in a sling?"

"It isn't obviously true to you that football players get special treatment when it comes to discipline and rule breaking?"

"I wouldn't know. I stay away from as much discipline as I can. Truth is, by the time they get enough goods on me to drag my ass to the office, there's not a lot of reasonable doubt. What's this article gonna be about, anyway?"

Montana lays her pen down on the table in exasperation. "I don't know. It seems to be taking off on me."

Trey nods toward the pen. "That mean we're taking a break?"

"For a minute. I have to gather my thoughts."

Trey picks up the pen and notebook. "I been thinking I might like this school paper thing. Lemme try it from your side."

"Actually, I'm asking the questions."

"Yeah, but you're taking a break. Weren't you a cheerleader back when I played JV, like when we were freshmen?"

Montana nods. "Yes, Trey, I was a cheerleader."

"You didn't get elected cheerleader wearing all that black shit, and all the *inserts*."

"You mean my piercings?"

"Yeah," he says. "Your piercings. In fact we had you on the fast track. Great legs, better . . . uh . . . torso, eight and a half face, maybe three percent body fat."

"The fast track to what?"

"Feminine superstardom," Trey says. "But you veered off on us. In a couple of simple sentences, so my fourth-grade level readers can understand, can you tell us why?"

"I can tell you in one simple sentence. Because you guys had me on the fast track."

"Is it true you have a tattoo on your abs of a bird pulling a worm out of your belly button?"

Montana snatches her pen back, blushing only slightly. "Back to the interview." She opens the notebook to her original page. Trey sits back. She says, "You say *you* don't get special treatment as a jock, and specifically as a football player. Would you say that in general, athletes get special treatment?"

"Of course I wouldn't say it. You want me to rat out my buddies on the gravy train?"

"So you're saying it's true, you just won't say it."

"A good journalist does not put words into the subject's mouth."

Football players are supposed to be jerks in Montana West's judgment, but Trey Chase is fun. She wouldn't admit this to anyone, but the way he plays her feels *sexy*.

"You know this is all on the record, right?"

"Yeah. Hey, would you like to go out for a Coke or a coffee or something? You know, sometime when you're not doing anything?"

"Uh, I don't know . . . uh . . . sure . . . sometime."

"How about sometime today after practice?"

"That's sometime, all right."

"It's a date, then. You gonna ask me any more questions?"

"Later, maybe. This interview is hard to control."

Trey says, "Anything that's too easy ain't worth doing."

Montana smiles. "That's not what I hear about you and your stable of girlfriends." She closes her notebook, winks, and gets up.

"You are not going on a date with Trey Chase."

"Okay," Montana says, "then I'm going out for coffee with Trey Chase."

Maxwell West sets down his fork and pinches the bridge of his nose. "The only time Trey Chase has coffee is in the morning. For a hangover. Trey Chase is what we used to call an ass bandit."

Montana almost spits her milk.

"Maxwell! There's a little girl at this table."

Tara looks up, smiles. That's *her*.

"Who has no idea of the meaning of what I just said." He turns back to Montana. "And what are you doing going out with a football player anyway? I thought you hated football players."

"Maybe I was being a bigot," Montana says, and shakes her head in disgust. "I'm doing a story on the football team."

"*You're* doing a story on the football team? That'll be the day. Maybe two years ago, before you started dressing like the Wicked Witch of the West."

"Don't be unkind, Daddy," she says. "The Wicked

Witch of the West isn't the only person who dresses in black."

"Darth Vader," he says.

"Catwoman," she says back.

"You can go out with any other football player you want, but you are not going out with Trey Chase." Maxwell West has never figured out that the best, fastest way to create his worst nightmare is to identify it.

She should never have said she was going out with Trey. She should have said she was meeting one of the guys on the football team to do a story on him because her control-freak right-wing Christian father—who is also chairperson of the school board—and his evil elves Remington and Holden won't let her write anything of substance. *That's* a better fight. Now she's stuck doing the two things she does best when it comes to her father.

"My dad didn't want me to meet you."

"Why not?" Trey and Montana are sitting in Connie's, a cup of steaming coffee on the table in front of each. Trey takes a small flask from his jacket pocket and pours a splash into his coffee, holds it up as an offering.

"He says you're an ass bandit. No thanks," she says to the bottle.

He smiles and returns it to his pocket.

"Did you tell your dad we don't call superstuds that anymore? So how'd you get to come out?"

"I lied." She nods toward the bottle. "Can't that get you thrown off the team?"

"Only if a rat sees me with it," he says. "Or if it shows up in the school paper."

She smiles. "And if it shows up in the school paper, my butt's in a sling because I'm not supposed to be out with you."

"Because I'm an ass bandit."

She nods.

"All the bases are covered."

They sip their coffees, and Montana feels uneasy, which is not normal; Montana West operates *in* control. But Trey is different; different from what she expected from a run-of-the-mill jock, and different from anyone she has met. This guy is, likc, unflappable, and he doesn't lead with his jock status or his muscle. He looks over at the counter, brings out the flask again. "Sure you don't want a little cream and sugar?"

She pushes her coffee toward him. "Just a little."

He smiles and pours a splash into her cup.

She sips. Smooth.

"So seriously, West, what are you doing writing an article on me, or on football?"

"Not that you're not interesting," Montana says, "but they won't let us print anything of *substance*. I had this great article on medical marijuana, but Remington told Conroy it was too controversial for a school paper. He claims the medical marijuana issue is a trick to legalize it so every pothead in the country gets a free ride."

"That right? Wonder if he's against medical OxyContin, or medical morphine? I should introduce you to my grandmother."

"Why's that?"

"You'll see." He leans his chair back on two legs. "So really, West, why the big change? You were a perfect match for this football culture."

"I was, wasn't I?"

He raises his eyebrows.

"It was too hard and it's stupid, a waste of time," she says. "When you're playing Lilac Queen, you spend half your life plucking your eyebrows and finding the right lipstick for the right outfit and for that matter, looking for the right outfit." She looks at the table. "And I didn't like the expectations."

"The fast track, huh. Don't blame you."

"To tell the truth, it was more the expectations at home. You can never be just right enough for my dad. He gives me a hard time now, but it was worse when he wanted my hair a little different, or was worried that I was showing a little too much boob, or that too much makeup made me look like a whore but too little made me look like I didn't care. He's such a prick. I saw how it had killed my mother and I figured, hey, I'm out of this."

"Your ol' man *is* kind of a dick." He points his finger at her like a pistol. "You kept the body, though."

Montana feels blood rush to her head.

"Some things you can't hide with loose clothes," he says.

"I stay in shape." She doesn't look at him; sits through an uneasy silence that is only uneasy to *her*.

"Hey," he says. "How long you got?"

She remembers the lie she told to get out, and her father's forbidding her to be here, at least with Trey Chase. "Long as I want."

"Wanna meet my grandmother?"

She laughs. "You're taking me home to meet the family already?"

"She'd like you," he says. "Follow my pickup."

■ ■ ■

"My grandson tells me you're doing a story on him for the school paper."

"Yes, ma'am."

"Must be a slow news week."

Montana sits at the kitchen table with Trey's grandmother; Mari Chase. She is a small woman, wiry and muscular, and her smooth face belies her sixty-plus years.

"I dabbled in some journalism in my day."

Montana thinks along with dabbling in journalism, she might have been a beauty "in her day." "Really?"

"A little paper called the *Berkeley Barb*."

"You wrote for the *Berkeley Barb*? Wasn't that like the biggest counterculture paper of the sixties?"

"That was the biggest counterculture paper of *all* time," Mari says. "In the late sixties, when the civil rights movement was cranked up and the war in Vietnam was headed into the shitter, the *Barb* was the place to get the real news, at least if you thought like we did."

"Hippies and stuff, right?" Montana says.

"See?" Trey says. "I *said* you had to meet my grandma."

"Wow," Montana says. "The *Berkeley Barb*."

"That's right, little girl. You have arrived at the heart of journalistic subterfuge." Mari leans against the table and coughs. "We had some fun. And we took care of a lot of people, including me. Max Scherr, who created the *Barb*, conscripted street kids to sell it. Flower children, we called ourselves." She smiles. "We *did* wear flowers in our hair, but a more accurate moniker might have been weed children."

No sweat figuring where Trey Chase gets his cool.

"We'd come in with something of value to use as collateral for some papers on the day it came out. If Max thought it was valuable enough that we'd come back for it, he'd give us a bundle to sell on the street. We'd return and buy our stuff back and there'd be enough left over for a new bundle to sell for food. I *loved* that paper. I started doing research for them and a little bit of editing. Finally he put me on staff."

"How did he pay to get it published? I mean, to print it up and all?"

"Sex ads," Mari says, shaking her head. "You should have read some of *those*. It was actually a pretty powerful newspaper at its peak. Max wasn't bound by the same constraints as, say, the *San Francisco Chronicle*. Once he printed a piece claiming dried banana skins contained bananadine, which would create an opium high if you smoked it. Totally made-up bullshit, but it found its way into the mainstream press, which caused a run on bananas in local supermarkets. There was actually an article in the *New York Times* on psychedelic substances, including banana skins. The Food and Drug Administration did an exhaustive study on them before declaring what Max knew all along. No psychedelics in banana skins." Mari is misty-eyed. "Those were the days."

"And I can't get an article published about gay marriage or assisted suicide. Just had the stops put on a really good article on medical marijuana."

Mari shoots a knowing glance at Trey. "No wonder my grandson doesn't like school. You're not going to sleep with him, are you?"

Montana blanches but recovers quickly. "I don't even know if I'll have coffee with him again."

"I hear that. He can be *such* a little prick. I'm afraid he has some of his mother's appetites, and about the same good sense for indulging them." She shakes her head. " I love him like no other, but somewhere between his hippie grandmother and his poly-addictive mother, neither of whom had a brain in her head when it came to mate selection, any sexual good sense that might have existed was lost."

"I'll remember that."

Trey smiles and shakes his head. "Grandma, you're making it hard to work my magic."

"That's my intention," his grandmother says. "I have opened the front door to face a tearful, jilted football-player-loving bimbo for the last time, if I have anything to say about it." She glances at Montana. "That's not you, dear. You seem different. But my grandson is a one-trick pony, and he uses that one trick on *all* the girls. Did it hurt when they pierced your cheek?"

"Not as much as you might think, and actually that's technically my upper lip. It's called a Marilyn," Montana says.

"A Marilyn."

"Yeah, it's in the same place Marilyn Monroe had her beauty mark. You've heard of Marilyn Monroe, right?"

Mari smiles. "Yes, dear. Marilyn Monroe and I share much of the same time in history."

"Oh, right. Anyway, the tongue was the tough one for me. Whoo. If I'd known it could ruin my teeth, I'd have never had it done. Plus I couldn't get used to it. I just wore it long enough to piss off my dad."

"How'd that work?"

Montana brightens. "Like a charm."

"I'm not surprised," Mari says. "Why don't you come out to the back porch with me?"

Montana rises, as does Trey. "You stay here, Trey. We're talking business."

Trey sits back down. "Your wish is my command."

"Don't forget that," his grandmother says.

On the porch Mari reaches into her purse to extract a doobie. Montana's eyes widen. "If you want an up-close and personal interview for your article on medical marijuana, I'm your girl."

Montana lets it register. "Are you . . . "

"Dying of cancer? Mmm-hmm."

"Oh, God, I'm sorry."

"Don't worry, honey, I'm fine with it. I've been resigned for a while. Trey turns eighteen in a month. I got him from where his mother blew him off to here. He still needs some work, obviously, but I swear, it's work for a younger girl." She nods toward Montana. "He's not really as bad as I let on, if you keep him on a short leash. In fact he has a lot more manners when he's on that leash. Remember that."

She lights the joint, inhales, and closes her eyes. "If those bastards had any idea the relief . . . " She takes another toke. "What arrogance. What . . . I'm sorry, dear. I didn't mean to get you involved in my radical left-wing politics."

"No, no, this is great stuff. I could stay out here with you all night."

"The best days of my life were my days on the

Barb," Mari says. "Showing the world what free speech was about. Actually I thought we cleared the road for you, but here we are, forty years later, afraid to hear the truth."

"So much for evolution," Montana says. "I guess things don't get better, they just swing back and forth."

"Know what you should do?"

"What?"

"You should write the hell out of that article. I'll interview for it. Submit it every week. What kind of balls does your teacher have?"

Montana laughs. No wonder Trey Chase talks the way he talks. "Dr. Conroy? Big. Way big."

"Would she fight for you?"

"She offered to take it to the school board. Course that's just taking it to my dad."

"You don't have to win to win," Mari says. "Just keep putting it in front of them. The truth rises."

"I like that," Montana says.

"Tell you what, you get your teacher to take that article to the school board, and I'll be there; make the case for *content*."

"But if you're sick . . . "

"If I'm sick, that would make my appearance all

the better," Mari says. "You don't mind taking on your father?"

Montana laughs. "That makes *me* feel all better."

"Your grandmother's pretty sick, huh?" Montana and Trey stand beside her car in front of Trey's house.

"Yeah, pretty sick."

"I'm sorry."

"Me, too," he says. "She doesn't deserve this. It is an ugly way to go."

"Anything I can do?"

"You could go to bed with me." He smiles and raises his eyebrows.

"Anything else?"

"One thing at a time."

Montana smiles and pecks him on the cheek. "We'll see." She slides into the driver's side of her car, clicks her seat belt, and squeezes his hand through the open window.

When Montana opens the door three minutes before her curfew, she spots Tara's suitcase sitting near the wall to the right. Her mother sits at the kitchen table, head in hands. Her father is nowhere to be seen.

Her mother doesn't look up as Montana enters the

kitchen. "I can't do it, Montana. She has to go back."

"What happened?"

"She doesn't want to be here. Whatever I tell her not to do is what she does. Her promises don't last a day. She's into everything. Nothing is private. It's like she has to know *everything* that's going on. The more I try to be her mother, the more she fights me."

"So you're giving her away?"

"I called the social worker, said I needed to take Tara back to the therapist. I guess I sounded more upset than I thought. Your father heard me from the other room, snatched the phone out of my hand, and told the social worker to come get her."

"But she's still here, right? They didn't come."

"She's in her room."

"Where's Daddy?"

"He's in our room."

"Mom, you're *not* going to give her up."

"I have no choice. I tried to back out, and your father said he wouldn't hear another word about it. That was it. I picked up the phone to call the social worker"—her voice cracks—"he raised his hand to—"

"To what? That bastard."

"I don't think he would have. It's been a long time."

"Then tell him too bad," says Montana. "Why does he get the last word? He didn't want her in the first place. You were the one who brought her here."

"There's nothing I can do, Montana. He won't budge."

Under her breath, Montana says, "He'll budge if you make it worth it."

"I hope I didn't hear what I think I heard."

Don't turn it back on *me*. "How does he always get his way?"

"Your father is the breadwinner, dear. He's the reason we have all this."

"So what if he died?"

"He's not going to die."

"You're probably right. No such luck," Montana says. "But he could. What if he did?"

"Don't be foolish. There's insurance, and I would get a job. We'd get by."

"That's my point. He works out in the world and you work here, and you work just as hard as he does. Shit, taking care of *me* is a full-time job. What if you told him Tara was staying and if he didn't like it *he* could go?"

Her mother hasn't, and wouldn't, *consider* that.

"I'm sorry, Montana. They're picking her up tomorrow."

Montana stands. "I hate you." She whirls and walks out of the room.

"Hey, little sis." Montana stands in the doorway to Tara's dark room.

"They're givin' me away," Tara says.

Montana moves in, sits on the side of the bed. "What did you do?"

"Nothin'."

"Was nothin' poop related?"

"Maybe. Prob'ly."

"Tara, why do you keep doing that?"

Tara buries her face in the pillow and starts to cry. "I get *mad*," she says.

"I know, but when *I* get mad, I scream and call names and kick things," Montana says. "I don't crap in secret places. Remember, we talked about this." She wants Tara to say it.

"They won't let me take care of nothin'," she says. "Greg messed up our family. He always got mad and didn't want to be waked up. You know what always happened with him? He didn't know the rule about no hitting. He should have to sit on the bed when he hurts me. He'd be there a long time. I wish I could have a great dad, like a new dad. He'd be nice to me. He wouldn't fight with my mom and me. He'd love us. Greg hit me and put me in the room. He locked Norman in the closet. Norman is better off with Grandma because she knows how to not hit him. It was hard for my mom and Greg. They would fight and then I'd have to be the boss and try to stop them. My mom would put methamphetamine in her or dope an' beer an' I'd take care of her. I think about her all the time. Where is she? Who's takin' care of her? I get scared nobody's takin' care of her. So I get mad an' then I'm poopin' someplace."

Tara isn't even poopin' on the Wests. She's poopin' on people she hasn't seen in months. She's doing what Montana did all those years ago, and still sometimes does; aching for that mom, that *first* mom; the one none of us sheds completely. She scoops Tara up; holds her to her chest.

Tara sobs. "They're givin' me away."

Montana holds and rocks her. No, by God, they are not givin' you away. If they give you away, they're givin' me away. She lets Tara cry herself to sleep before tiptoeing out and back to the kitchen.

"I won't let you do it, Mom."

"Montana, it is *done*. I don't want to hear another word. Your father—"

"Fuck my father," she says, and her mother stands and slaps her face.

"And fuck *you*!" she screams. "If she goes, I go!" And even louder. "YOU HEAR ME, DADDY? IF SHE GOES, I GO! You guys don't even know what's wrong with her!"

The quick, heavy pounding of Maxwell West's shoes on the stairs is followed by his appearance in the kitchen doorway, the vein in his forehead pulsating. "What's going on down here? What is the matter with you? Did I hear you say what I think you said?"

Montana stands defiant. "You heard what you heard. What makes you God? At home you take in a little girl, and when the going gets tough, you dump her. I can't get published in my own school newspaper because the big almighty president of the school board who happens to be my dad will back up the gutless idiots who run that place. Well, that's fine. I'll write stupid articles about the football team and the prom and what horrible pressure is put on us by college entrance testing. You can be the fucking power-freak-monger out in the world all you want. Out there it just makes people hate you. But you throw a kid away and you're breaking something that doesn't get fixed. You know I'm right, and you don't care. But if you get rid of Tara, I go with her!"

Maxwell's voice goes soft and dangerous. "You listen to me, young lady. You may talk like that in front of your friends, but I will *not* have you talking like that in my house."

Montana's eyes narrow, and she grits her teeth. "You're about to ruin a little girl's life and all you care about is me saying fuck?" She turns to her mother. "You know what Tara said to me? She said she needs you to make her mad. So she can *be* mad. She needs you to let her feel the way she feels instead of trying to control her. Nobody has any control around here, and you know why? Because *he* has it all. I had to turn into a bitch to survive, and tell you what, Mom, you better do the same. You better stand up to him or you're going to shrivel up and die."

"Montana . . . "

"You know I'm right."

"You want to know why Tara's going back?" Maxwell asks. "Because I swore I would *never again* go through what I went through with you. Do you know how close we came to giving you up?"

"I know how close you are right now," Montana says. "I'll be eighteen in three weeks. If I come home from school tomorrow and Tara isn't here, I'm *gone*. And I will spend the rest of my time in this stinking town getting even with you. I promise I will."

"You leave and you'll get *nothing* from us," Maxwell says. "There will be no money for college, there will be no allowance, there will be no car, there will be no *nothing*."

"If you give her up, I wouldn't take a bag of Cheetos from you."

"You'd be smart to go to your room before you say something you can't take back. This conversation is over."

Montana turns back to her mother, who sits silent, staring at the table. Montana kneels in front of her. "When you guys go to bed tonight and ask each other if I'll really do it, I'm telling you, my word is gold. I will take my stuff, and I will hate you for the rest of my life."

She stalks to her room.

When Montana sees Tara standing defiant in that corner, she's looking straight into history. She knows no matter how Tara tries, when she feels like that, it goes one way; a handful of poop where it doesn't belong. The only explanation is, "I get *mad*." What's happening to Tara now might as well be happening to *her*, and Maxwell West has put himself in her sights. It boils down to the Maxwell Wests of the world, from blocked newspaper articles to "You are *not* going out with Trey Chase" to "If you leave here you won't get a thing" to a throwaway six-year-old girl. She visualizes her mother sitting at that table, defeated, and she wants to slap her into the next county.

It's everywhere. Remington and Holden are simply Maxwell Lite; second and third verse, same as the first. If she takes them on, she ends up at the school board meeting, where *he* wields the gavel. But what the hell. Why not? Mari was right; you don't have to win.

"You can stay at my place if you want," Trey says. The two stand next to Montana's locker.

"Right. I'm going to stay at your place after you've already propositioned me."

"Listen, the safest place in the world for you, if you don't want me in your pants, is at my grandmother's place. I'd run into two-hundred-thirty-pound linebackers all day before I'd let her catch me getting birthday suited up with a girl in her house."

"I was going to ask Dr. Conroy. . . . "

"She's a teacher. She'll have to get permission from your parents, or go through some legal bullshit to make it cool, and in the end, Maxwell West gets his hooks into it. A lot of work for a place to crash."

"You sure she won't mind?"

"You got a cell phone?"

Montana pulls it out of her purse, drops it in his extended hand. He dials. "Grandma . . . Trey . . . I know, but you answered anyway. . . . You're right, it could have been a telemarketer. You could have bought me something cool. Listen, would it be okay if Montana stays with us for a while? . . . I don't know, a *while* . . . No, no, none of that . . . Yup, the room farthest from mine . . . "

He holds the cell against his leg. "You're not on the run, are you?"

Montana shakes her head.

Into the phone: "Nope, Grandma, she's just leaving home, and she's close enough to eighteen, by the time they got it sorted out . . . All right, she'll probably come over after school. I'll see you after practice."

"Reservation for one at the Hotel Mary Jane," he says, and hands Montana back her cell.

Dr. Conroy waits in Principal Remington's office. He will be returning from lunch presently. She has ten minutes before the bell and feels the urge to get this issue into the open. He will be angry, or at least petulant. They've been through this, but Montana wants one more shot and is willing to face her father at the school board. She expects him to lay the blame one step above him, so she will have this meeting twice today; once with Mr. Remington and once with Dr. Holden. The answer will be the same, and she will request time at the next school board meeting. Holden will say the school board is drowning in business, and Dr. Conroy will say she will be more than happy to wait till the end of the meeting but they should probably schedule a good bit of time because there will likely be students present. Holden will threaten; Dr. Conroy will remind him she has tenure and is doing this by the numbers. At some point within a month, they will have a hearing on Montana West's article on medical marijuana.

Ah, public education.

"Hey, Trey, could you take me over to Social and Health Services during lunch?"

"You can get a better sandwich at Subway," Trey says, turning to shove his backpack into his locker, "but sure. You applying for Social Security?"

"Huh-uh," Montana says. "I'm gonna try to find my little sis. Mrs. Crummet—she's Tara's social worker— said she'd be happy to talk with me."

"A social worker will talk to a kid?"

"That's what they *do*, dummy." She punches him

playfully on the shoulder. Trey has kept his promise to his grandmother to stay away from Montana's room and to refrain from openly obvious manipulations to get her out of her clothes. Montana has failed to do the same, however, and they are in danger of creating a seriously malevolent grandma. So far, they've been more cautious than Mari's been vigilant.

"You think they'll let you see her?"

"It depends on how she's doing in her new placement," Montana says. "If things are going smoothly they won't, but if she's the same toilet on wheels she was at our place—at the *Wests'* place—they'll let me see her in hopes it will calm her down. It'll be up to the family. Hey, I know this system inside out. I operated undercover for years."

"Did a little stint myself," Trey says.

"Serious?"

"You notice there's a generation gap between me and my grandma. Grandma says she played it way too loose with Mom." He laughs. "It's taken my family a good long while to learn to control all the uncontrollable substances Grandma got into. My mom was like, all messed up when she had me, and I was born with a positive meconium drug screen. You know what that is?"

"Sure do. It means your momma was treating herself

as your bong, getting you high before you ever saw the light of day."

"I didn't lose her, though, like you did," Trey says. "We both got placed with Grandma, and when Grandma finally placed my mother somewhere else, I was all for it."

"That's funny."

"So I take my anger out on linebackers and you take yours out in bed."

"Oh, ha! I'll show you anger."

"She's having a hell of a time," Sandra Crummet says to Montana over the table in the interview room at the Department of Social and Health Services. "She's bossing them around, wandering the house at night like a Village of the Damned kid. They had to put an alarm on her door. She's chewing on the back of the couch. It's only temporary, but frankly we're not having much luck finding a foster-adopt. Tara comes with quite a résumé."

"Did you try to get my parents to reconsider?"

Sandra chuckles and shakes her head. "Of course. The first two tries I got your father, who wouldn't let me talk to your mother. He told me to stop calling because he forbade your mother to change her mind."

"The Great Forbidder."

"Anyway, I figured out his crazy work hours and got through to your mom, but I had zero luck. She said you were gone, too. Is that true?"

"I told them Tara and I were a package."

Sandra stares at her knees and shakes her head. "This system puts a lot of stress on folks. If it makes you feel any better, Tara keeps asking for you."

Tears well in Montana's eyes. "It makes me feel worse."

Sandra pats her hand. "Well, we'll see what we can do."

"Listen," Montana says. "Tell the foster parents to give her some things to be in control of. When she gets all bossy and shit, don't just take everything away. It's not personal. I'm telling you, once you're like that, you're like that. You can't make it go away because people tell you it's not good for you. Remember how you guys used to call me parentified?"

Sandra laughs. "God, yes. You were the best four-year-old mom I ever saw. And when your adoptive mother would try to take all your ''sponsibilities' away from you, you pooped in the dryer."

"Well, I'm still like that. God, Sandy, *anybody* pushes me around, I come at 'em like a banshee. I know that's why I hate my dad so much."

Sandra smiles, throwing up her hands.

"I'm not kidding you, Sandy. Tell the foster parents to give her things to do. And tell them not to worry if Tara makes them feel like shit. *She* feels like shit, and she needs the company."

"That's not easy to explain," Sandra says.

"Want me to talk to them?"

Sandra looks Montana up and down, from piercing to piercing to black jacket to waist chain to black pants. "Yeah. Maybe you can show them your worm tattoo while you're at it," she says. "No, dear, this is not a family who wants to hear from Batgirl."

"You know," Trey says on the way back to school, "there's this woman my grandmother plays poker with who's raised at least a dozen foster kids. She doesn't have any now, but she might go for one more, if Grandma lets her win once in a while."

"Serious?"

"Yeah, you should hear some of the stories this woman tells. I listened to her one night when the game was at our place. Some of the kids she took in would make Tara look like Joan of fucking Arc."

"Wait. Wasn't Joan of Arc crazy?"

"That's one theory," Trey says, "but she was crazy good. These kids were crazy bad."

■ ■ ■

"You want to bring me up to speed?" Dr. Conroy and Montana sit at the large table in the journalism room, working on the final touches of the layout for the paper.

"On what?"

"I hear you're out of your house, living with the Chases? Is that right?"

Montana blushes slightly. "Uh-huh."

"I thought you hated football players. Is this situation chaperoned?"

"It's chaperoned," she says, leaving out "*except when we're fucking.*"

Dr. Conroy watches her, brow furrowed.

"Trey's grandma is a mother bear," Montana says. "You don't have a thing to worry about."

"Well, if I *did* have something to worry about, it wouldn't be that you guys don't use protection, would it?"

"No, ma'am." Finally, something she can be truthful about.

"You make sure it stays that way."

"Yes, ma'am."

"I got the revised version of your medical marijuana article." She holds it up. "I haven't had a chance to read it yet, but I went to see Mr. Remington. The wheels are grinding again, but he is pretty upset with me. Did you add to this? It looks longer than before."

"A little. There's an interview. Wait till you read it."

"I'll look it over, for all the good it will do. You know what Holden will say."

Montana nods again. "Yup, but the faster we get their answers, the faster we get back to the school board."

Dr. Conroy watches her a moment more. "How much of this is about you not living at home? Is this a vendetta?"

"A what?"

Dr. Conroy looks toward the closed door. In a lower voice, she says, "A 'fuck you.'"

"No. Well, maybe a little." She nods. "Maybe a lot."

"I'm not willing to put the school paper in the middle of personal business between you and your father," Dr. Conroy says.

"It won't look personal, I promise. Dr. Conroy, he has to have everything his way. My mother just caves and does what he says. My foster sister has to find a new home because my dad doesn't like to be inconvenienced; nobody ever stands up to him. Maxwell West says this, Maxwell West says that, and it just happens. He'll talk to the rest of the school board members before he even opens this meeting. *Jesus* could present our case and He'd lose. I don't expect to see my article in print, but the word will get out when the paper covers the meeting."

"Do you want to see your room?" Montana crouches before Tara, standing in the doorway with a paper sack filled with clothes.

"Uh-huh."

"It's the best one," Montana says. "It has the biggest window of all the bedrooms and a brand-new bed. Whenever you come to visit, you'll have all your own stuff."

"Do you got a room?"

"Right across the hall from yours," Montana says. "So, like, if you get scared, you can just run over and crawl in bed with me. Like when we were at home."

Trey stands behind Montana, whispers in her ear: "Unless you don't happen to be in there."

Montana ventriloquists back, "When she's here I *will* be in there."

"I'm starting to hate this kid already."

Tara says, "Can I live here all the time?"

"Huh-uh," Montana says. "You have a new mom

and she doesn't want to give you up because you are so cool. But I get to baby-sit, and you can come stay here if you miss me. And you always get to come when your new mom comes over to play poker with Trey's grandma."

"What's poker?"

Mari, now standing in the doorway, says, "That's when your new momma comes over here to play cards and I take all her money."

Tara stares.

"Don't worry, honey. I'll give some of it back to her so she can buy you food."

Montana puts a hand on Tara's shoulder. "You know where you're pooping, right?"

"In the toilet."

"And what are you going to do when you get mad?"

"Be a bitch."

Montana blushes slightly, smiles at Trey.

He says, "Peer mentoring?"

"We need to make sure you have a job when you're over here," Mari says, following Montana's earlier advice. "Do you want a job?"

Tara nods enthusiastically.

"Okay," Mari says, looking askance at Montana and

Trey, "you're in charge of population control. This is a very important job. If you see Montana and Trey kissing too much, you know, like, if it gets *icky*? You bug them. Make them play with you. If they won't, scream and yell and go all off."

"You mean be a bitch?"

"Exactly," Mari says. "And if you see them sneaking to Montana's room, which is right next to yours, be twice as much a bitch. See, my grandson and your sister think nobody pays enough attention to them around here. You're going to change that. Is that a job you think you can do?"

"That's a good job," Tara says. "I can do it."

"Can you cook?"

Tara's eyes brighten. "Yup," she says. "I used to cook for my mom. She put drugs in her all the time. When you put drugs in you, sometimes you forget dinner."

"Well, I don't put drugs in me," Mari says, well aware she *inhales* drugs when the need arises. "But I need plenty of help anyway. Lord knows I'm old as sin. Think we should get some dinner started? Here, I got you this apron." She hands Tara a red apron embroidered with a cook wearing a high chef's hat and brandishing a rolling pin, above the caption BOSS OF YOU IN MY KITCHEN."

■ ■ ■

Students and citizens pour into the parking lot at the high school and stream into the cafeteria as the clock nears seven in the evening, nearly three weeks after Dr. Holden has upheld the censorship of Montana's medical marijuana article. She might have had a better shot with the gay marriage piece, but this one covers more bases. Other than a chance meeting at a local restaurant, she hasn't seen her father since she stomped out to live with the Chases. She has purposely avoided him in order to keep her disgust and contempt quotients as high as possible. It takes as much anger as she can muster to battle the intimidation she can't help but feel. Maxwell West is a *force*. As much as she hates to admit it, she understands why her mother never stands up to him. You have to get *cranked* up, and her mother doesn't have the crank. Montana does.

Maxwell opens the meeting asking for a motion to table the reading of the minutes from the last meeting and the old business. "We have a large number of students and citizens interested in the school newspaper issue, and if there are no objections I'd like to get to that. I believe it can be cleared up rather quickly, but in the event that I've underestimated, I'd like everyone to get home at a decent hour. It *is* a school night."

That brings a moderate laugh.

"Let me see if I can sum up the situation," Maxwell says. "If I leave anything out, I'd appreciate someone filling it in. A senior student in the journalism class has written an investigative piece, or an op-ed piece, I'm not sure which, promoting the virtues of medical marijuana. In the interest of full disclosure, that student happens to be my daughter, which you already know. I don't expect it to be germane to our discussion. Dr. Amanda Conroy, who teaches the journalism class and is also the faculty adviser to the newspaper, is advocating for Miss West. At the principal level and at the superintendent level, the decision has been made not to run the story. The school board level, *this* level, is the last stop. I'd like to hear from Dr. Conroy and Dr. Holden first, and then I believe we have members of the community and students who wish to speak." Maxwell looks at Dr. Conroy and Dr. Holden, seated in the front row. "Did I miss anything?"

"I don't believe you did, Max," Dr. Holden says.

Dr. Conroy says, "No, sir."

"Who wants to go first?"

The two nod at each other, hesitate. Holden says, "I'll do the honors." He stands, walks to the lectern and faces the sizeable crowd, speaking with no notes. "It is

····

137

our job to provide our students with the best education we can. We have to provide the fundamentals and we have to take our more capable students as far on their educational journey as possible before releasing them into the world. We have state standards to meet and in this school's case, state standards to surpass. We have to look to the needs of *all* the students first, and then to the needs of the community. In other words, we have a lot of people to please. It's a juggling act. If we allow our students to print anything they please in the school newspaper, it will get ugly quick, and pretty soon many of you here tonight in support of Dr. Conroy and Montana West will be in my office screaming for the administration to get control. The school newspaper represents our school to the community, in the same way our athletic teams and our music program do. Our athletes wear coats and ties when they represent us officially, and our band and orchestra wear clean, pressed, impeccable uniforms. We're only asking the same of the school newspaper.

"It is the community that decides, with their votes, whether or not we can keep our nonessential programs. Quite frankly I don't care to preside over a school district that includes only bare educational essentials because we have offended so many community members that we can't pass a school bond issue. Miss West's article on medical marijuana is well written, let there be no mistake. But we all know the medical marijuana issue is a thinly veiled plan to legalize marijuana so it can be used by the masses. The slipperiest of slopes. Board members have been given a copy of the article, and you will note that Miss West makes no mention of the true nature of the controversy. Given the dangerous nature of drug and alcohol use in our teenage culture today, both Mr. Remington and I felt the issue should be excluded from the list of accepted subject matter for our school paper. Our job is to teach students the *process*. Objectionable-content material can be addressed later, in a college or university newspaper, or in a real newspaper. As soon as Dr. Conroy has made her statements, I'll be more than happy to answer questions."

Dr. Conroy replaces Holden at the podium, formally acknowledges the board and the audience.

"Dr. Holden and I have been having this 'discussion,' which often appears like an argument, since I took over the school newspaper. Being a journalist by trade and by nature, I of course see this as an intellectual freedom issue. A First Amendment issue. I try to teach my students not only *how* to write a good article—be it objective news or editorial opinion—but how to choose *what* articles to write. I teach them to be topical, to attend to the issues of the day, and to follow their interests. We do live in a free country where the free flow of controversial ideas and opinions is supposed to be celebrated. In censoring Montana's article due to content, or her earlier article on the gay marriage controversy, or her op-ed piece on teenage abortion, we censor that free flow of ideas. Simple as that. I too will be more than happy to take questions from the audience. Thank you." Dr. Conroy returns to her seat.

Maxwell West directs those who wish to speak to line up behind a microphone set up in the aisle. Both students and parents approach. He gives them a time limit of two minutes each.

Students side nearly unanimously with Dr. Conroy. They live in a free country and that includes being able to say what they want. A number of adults agree. An equal number do not. They believe school should be a *controlled* environment, where subject material is chosen with restraint. Students are not "full-fledged citizens," as one man puts it, and need guidance. It is the responsibility of the community and the school to provide oversight when it comes to controversial and dangerous ideas.

All in all, most would agree it is a civil discourse,

although on a couple of occasions Maxwell has to bring the gavel down hard when students boo the idea that they're not ready to take *responsibility* for what they express.

With everyone heard, Maxwell calls for a recess while the board discusses it. In fifteen minutes, the meeting is called back to order. "The board has come to a decision," he says when all are seated. "We hire administrators because of, among other things, their capacity to make good judgments in difficult situations. We think we've made great hires in Mr. Remington as principal and Dr. Holden as superintendent. We also think we made a great hire in Dr. Conroy as an English and journalism teacher and as adviser to the school paper. Students come out of her classes with wonderful skills. In this case, however, we have to agree with Dr. Holden. This is not really a First Amendment issue because the cold hard truth is, if you're not eighteen in this country, you don't have any rights, so while it's a point well taken, it's not really germane."

Boos drown out everything after "you don't have any rights," but Maxwell brings down the gavel, and they finally die out. "Whether you like that or not, it's the truth. We as administrators and school board have to make hard decisions about what keeps our kids safe, because in the end, that's what it's all about. We can choose to be your *friends* and abide by your wishes, or we can choose to be the guiding adults in your lives and risk our popularity with you. We would rather have you safe, and angry with us, than like us, and be at risk. The medical marijuana article will not be published in the school paper, and the administrators will continue to monitor what does or does not make it into that paper. I'd like to thank you all—"

"Excuse me." Trey Chase stands at the podium in the aisle.

"Actually, young man, the period for community input has passed," Maxwell says. "If you—"

"I know, and I apologize, but I didn't know the part about students' rights. I just have a quick question."

After a moment of consideration and a perturbed sigh, Maxwell says, "Go ahead."

"I turned eighteen yesterday," Trey says. "Do I have any rights?"

"Actually, technically—"

"Naw, man. You said people under the age of eighteen don't have rights. I'm eighteen. A bunch of us are; you know, held back because our parents wanted us to be great jocks in our senior years, or because we didn't put the ol' nose to the grindstone in third grade. But there are a lot of eighteen-year-olds in this school.

Do we have rights? Would it be different if *I* wrote that article? Hard to imagine me being part of an *intellectual freedom* issue, but would I have been?"

Maxwell considers a moment. "Actually, no. You're still part of a system that you started into as a child. You are in the care of that system, and it is a system designed for children in the technical sense of the word. A person paying child support pays until the child is out of school, even if that child turns eighteen before graduation. It's the same principle. Until you complete the process, you are under the tutelage of that system."

"Are you just making shit up?" Trey says.

"Young man! That language is totally inappropriate for this meeting."

"You're right," Trey says, hands up in surrender. "I apologize. Are you just making stuff up?"

"No, I'm not. Now a decision has been reached, and this meeting—"

"Excuse me." Trey's grandmother has slipped in behind him at the podium.

Maxwell says, "Yes?"

"I'm Mari Chase, this foul-mouthed teenager's grandmother."

"Our meeting is—"

"I know, I know," Mari says. "But I'm slow like

my grandson, and there's a lot I didn't understand until tonight. Plus, I need to apologize for his foul mouth. I apologize for that a lot. We've spent the evening talking law; what each of us can and can't do legally. But we're forgetting there's a *reason* people want to be heard, and it's the reason we have the First Amendment. It's personal, about each of us being able to stand up for what we believe in. The First Amendment was created by real humans to address a real problem. At the time, the problem was called tyranny. This little girl wrote an article about medical marijuana. A few moments ago, you said everyone knew that trying to legalize marijuana for medical purposes was the first step down the slippery slope to legalizing it for everyone, intimating that both the article and the proposed legislation are frivolous."

Maxwell nods, waits.

"I have cancer. If you hold this meeting this time next year, I likely will be absent. Marijuana eases my pain considerably; it makes life tolerable, but I can't get it without breaking the law. I could get specific about my discomfort, but I didn't come here for sympathy. You know, you and I agree on one thing; as long as it's a law, if I score some weed I'm going to be, and *should* be, arrested. But laws don't get changed at school board meetings. Laws get changed because people use their rights to express their opinions in public in order to *change the public's opinion.* Your dau—excuse me, Montana West, wrote this article because she believes that I and people like me shouldn't have to suffer at the end of our lives, and that the law ought to protect us, just as you believe the law has to protect these kids from knowing truths that many of them are going to run into within a year."

Maxwell is still another moment. And another. Then, "Your point is well taken." He nods at Trey. "As is *yours.* But we've made our ruling, and I'm afraid this meeting is over."

If nearly anyone in attendance were asked at what point the meeting got out of hand, they would agree, right when Maxwell West said, "This meeting is over." Suddenly he is standing face-to-face with his adopted daughter at the podium, inches from his microphone. "You're not getting away with this, Daddy. You *have* to be right! You don't care one bit if you really are. You'll do anything to look good. I'm out of your house, Tara is out of your house, all because it's more important for you to be right than to be true." The crowd falls silent as Montana's voice echoes through the room. Maxwell reaches for the switch on the

mike, but Montana snatches it away. She quotes
from memory material from the article that has been
successfully censored. "People in constant pain from
cancer, people who will end that pain with their deaths,
can't have any comfort because control freaks like you
don't want to be *tricked* by a bunch of potheads into
legalizing a drug that doesn't do half the harm as the
two drinks of Scotch you had tonight before you came
here."

Again Maxwell reaches for the mike, and again
Montana holds it out of his reach. He grabs her
shoulder.

"What are you going to do, Daddy, hit me? Go ahead.
I'm not giving you this mike. If you have something to
say, speak up."

The crowd remains silent, staring. Maxwell stares
back.

"Speak up, Daddy. Tell them why you're willing to
let people suffer just so you can look good."

"You listen here, you ungrateful little . . . Don't you
try to get these people thinking I'm some kind of monster
because you can't get your way with me or because you
can't get that foolish article published. And don't try
to pretend that you don't *look* for things to write about
that you know will offend decent people. You look for

trouble, and you get trouble. That's what this is really about. You find a teacher to back you—always one that thinks it's more important to be your friend than your guide—then you try to make those of us holding a moral standard for our school and our community look like monsters." Maxwell's face is flushed, and he begins to stammer.

Take a look, John and Jane Public, Montana thinks. This is what Maxwell West looks like when he can't have control.

She goes for the kill, again referencing the article that will never see the light of day, but which will be talked about around town for a *long* time after this night.

"I don't have to try to make you look like monsters," she says. "You're worse than monsters. You don't even believe in the freedom you preach. Did you hear yourself a minute ago? You said, 'If you're under eighteen in this country, you don't have any rights.' My research says that's not exactly correct, but it also says you can probably get away with whatever you want if you're not challenged. But I don't get it. Why do you want us to live in an environment that isn't real? Every kid in this room will be an adult in four years or sooner. Every time you tell us we can't express ourselves after that, we can tell you to go to hell. Well, fine, Daddy. You win tonight. But you don't win the intellectual argument; you win a control-freak argument. You guys are all scared, and I know how scared you are by how red your face is and how much you wish you could hit me right now. Look at you; you're ready to explode. So like I said, you win, but I can still say it. Go to hell."

Maxwell West's eyes narrow. In a voice that is barely picked up by the microphone, he says, "We took you when nobody would take you, you little snot. We raised you as decently as we knew how. We gave you all of what you needed and most of what you wanted. We took you to church every week. And how do you repay us? You talk like a whore and you dress like a witch. A tramp witch. By God, understand this. I'm glad I had the good sense to get rid of Tara before she had a chance to grow up and ruin my household the way you did. I'm glad she's gone and I'm glad you're gone. I know how to return decency to my household and I know how to keep decency in the school. I took care of the former a month ago, and I'm taking care of the latter right now." He looks up at more than a hundred sets of eyes on him, seems disoriented a moment, then sets his jaw.

Montana turns to the still-silent crowd. "There you

have it, folks. There's the *real* guy you elected to your school board. On behalf of the student body of Bear Creek High, I'd like to say *thanks a lot!*"

The Bear Creek Barb
Op-Ed/Obituary
Thursday, April 7

Mari Chase died yesterday of cancer. She is survived by her grandson, Trey Chase, as well as Montana West, who considered Mari her guardian angel. Mari was only sixty-two years old. Foulmouthed, funny, and wise, she admittedly did a horrible job raising her own daughter, Asia. When Asia fell into a world of drug and alcohol abuse and domestic violence, Mari took her only son and tried to right the wrongs she had committed with Asia all those years ago; tried to stop the awful flood of dysfunction roaring down through her generations. She's gone now, but she did it. Trey Chase finished the year as the leading rusher on the state champion Bear Creek High School football team and has enrolled at Eastern Washington State University on a full football scholarship. He is quoted as saying he wants to play football, sleep with a lot of girls, and maintain his C- average through to graduation. His girlfriend, the above-mentioned Montana West and the author of this piece, is quoted as saying the C- average is a generous exaggeration, but if he wants to sleep with a lot of girls, he better get a lot tougher than he is because she's going to Eastern on a full academic scholarship and has promised to print the name of every girl he sleeps with in the *Easterner*, Eastern's soon-to-be highly touted newspaper.

Mari Chase was denied the legal use of medical marijuana to ease the constant pain of her disease for the last year and a half of her courageous life. But Mari was resourceful, and her grandson, who she fondly referred to as Dr. Chase when he presented her with her "filled prescription" at the beginning of each week, had an incredibly green thumb for a football player. "I've given up my license to practice," he said when confronted by this reporter with the random drug testing he will face at the university.

Several months ago, at a school board hearing on censorship for the Bear Creek High School newspaper, the president of the Bear Creek school board said, "If you're under eighteen in this culture, you have no rights." That statement was the basis for censoring an op-ed piece supporting the use of medical marijuana. What the president should have said is, "If you're a student at Bear Creek High School, you have no rights."

As the existence of this column, indeed this newspaper, makes evident, he was wrong.

Next Week: Read the first in Montana West's three-part investigative series on medical marijuana. And watch for her subsequent series on the overwhelmed child protection and foster care system and the children who fall victim to that system.

Remember, the money you spend for the Bear Creek Barb *adds to the college fund of the person who sells it. When you close your eyes each night in the warmth of your down comforter, remember that, though she has a college scholarship, the person who handed you this paper will get no help from her family with incidentals needed for a proper higher education. Heavy tipping is appreciated!*

Nak's Notes
First Impressions
Transcribed directly from digital recorder

NAME: *Matt Miller*

AGE: *17*

REASONS TO BE PISSED: *Well, hell, he's a teenager. That does it right there.*

SIGNIFICANT CHARACTERISTICS: *Plenty of self-esteem, articulate, intelligent, athletic, good-looking kid. What the hell is he doing here?*

COPING SKILLS: *Seems to have about all he needs.*

PROGNOSIS: *Gotta like his chances.*

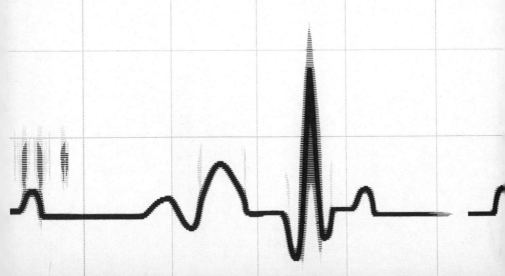

NAME: *Marcus James*

AGE: *17*

REASONS TO BE PISSED: *A gay black kid in the inland North-west. Shoot me.*

SIGNIFICANT CHARACTERISTICS: *Gay black kid in the inland Northwest. Gay black kid in the inland Northwest who's still standing. Big-time IQ. Helluva granddad. IQ. Lots of ambition. In your face.*

COPING SKILLS: *Sense of humor, ability to come right back at ya, Ivy League smart, on a good day knows to keep his head down.*

PROGNOSIS: *Who knows? If I was him I'd make tracks soon as I graduated.*

Meet Me at the Gates, Marcus James

Marcus

I walk into Mr. S's class after first lunch, late as usual, and slip into my seat in the back row.

"Mr. James. Nice of you to join us." Mr. S talks like that; says "Nice of you to join us" when he means "You're late again, Marcus."

"I'm in great demand," I tell him. "Got to spread myself thin sometimes."

"Well, spread yourself thicker," he says. "When you get to Stanford, your professors may not recognize your well-concealed brilliance the way I do. What is that around your neck?"

"That would be a noose, sir." I bring the knot from the back to the front and hold it up. "Nicely tied. Like it?"

"I don't like it and don't call me sir unless you mean it. Would you mind telling me why you're wearing a noose? Then would you mind taking it off before you get hauled down to The Bea . . . Mr. Bean's Office?"

"It was hanging on my locker," I tell him. "Whoever put it there must'a wanted me to wear it. It's one of the best I've seen, sir, and I've seen a few; I did a research paper.

Thirteen wraps. Nice and tight. Plus, it's pink. That's two birds with one rope. A lot of work went into this."

Mr. S gets all serious right quick. "That was hanging on your locker?"

"Yes, sir."

He is instantly jack-jawed; surveys the room. Like that? I said "surveys." This boy was perfect on his SAT verbals. "Who knows anything about this?"

I see Marshall and Strickland shoot each other a quick look across the room; everyone else stays turned at their desks, staring at me. I smile and nod.

Mr. S says, "This is a hate crime. You all know that, right?"

Marilyn Steelman says, "That's awful. That's just awful."

Marshall leans over to Ray Stone and whispers, "Oooooo. It's awful."

Mr. S walks to Marshall, who sits two desks over from me. "Did you have something to do with this, Roger?"

"No, sir. It's a hate crime." They lock eyes, and a whole bunch of air goes out of the room. Mr. S is one of the few teachers who doesn't cut Marshall some slack 'cause he's a stud ballplayer, and Marshall doesn't appreciate that. He'd bail on this class if it wasn't U.S. Government, which is required for him to graduate to his waiting career as a psycho-murderer and serial rapist.

"Stone?"

"No, sir. It's a hate crime."

Mr. S nods slowly and walks to Strickland's desk. "Aaron? You keepin' to the code like your buddies?"

"No code, sir. It's a hate crime."

It's pretty sure these guys did it, but it's possible not because they'd want you to think it even if it were somebody else's primo idea. You can tell Mr. S doesn't think we need to look further, but, innocent till proven you fucked up, you know; and this is U.S. Government, where supposedly that's not just an empty platitude. "Keep it civil till I get the library aide to come down and watch you hoodlums," he says to the class. "Come with me, Marcus."

"Man," I say. "They hang a noose on my locker and *I* go to the office. A gay black dude can't get a break in this town."

"A little less talk, a little more do, Marcus. Follow me." In the hall he says, "We're gonna get to the bottom of this."

"No bottom to get," I say. "If Marshall didn't do it, he threatened to take the life of the guy he made do it for him. No point goin' to see The Bean. Conference championship game in three weeks if they stay undefeated. Shee. Marshall could rape The Bean's daughter and he'd get one day in-home suspension. And that day would be a Sunday."

Mr. S says, "Yeah, well, we'll see about that."

We continue down the hall. "Man, if I'd known you were going to take me to The Bean, I might have put the brakes on my civil disobedience."

"I've got your back on this one, Marcus. We're going to be sure Mr. Bean knows the seriousness. Of course you know he'll make you take it off, right? Now that you've made your point."

Mr. S knows me, knows I like to make my point and then maybe make it again and maybe again after that to be sure everybody got it. When you are the single man or woman of color in a school of nine hundred and your sexual preference matches one out of ten, you figure ways to hold your own. One person of color went here before me, but he graduated a couple of years before my time. He didn't have Roger Marshall to deal with; he had his uncle, also a stud football player and also a man who liked to make other folks' lives risky.

When I don't answer, Mr. S says it again. "Uh, your point. You've made it, right Marcus?"

"You think?"

"You don't?"

"Let's see what The Bean thinks."

Mr. S shakes his head. "This isn't going the way I'd like. Do me a favor."

"Yeah?"

"Don't call him The Bean to his face."

"A noose."

"Yes sir. An' this here's a noose of a different color. Pink."

"On your locker."

"On my locker."

"Was there a note?" The Bean wants to know.

"It's a *noose*."

Mr. S closes his eyes and smiles.

"Tell you what, Mr. James, why don't you hand that over and we'll see what we can do about discovering who put it there."

Mr. S sports a grimace.

"Nah, I'll keep it," I tell him. "I wouldn't want it gettin' lost in the evidence room."

The Bean stiffens. "I'm not about to let you wear it outside this office, Mr. James."

"It was a *gift*, sir. It would be impolite not to wear it. Should you need it down the road, it'll be right here."

The Bean sucks big air and looks toward the ceiling. The Bean is known, on occasion, to explode. It is said he's learning to increase the interval between explosions; they can be embarrassing. I know how he wants this to go, and it ain't goin' that way. I walk around this school in somebody's crosshairs most of the time, and in this instance I think it's best to publicize the build-up to the possible crime against my person, in order to make the crime itself not happen. Expose the bad guys so if something happens to you, all eyes turn on them. My man MLK Jr. used to do that and . . . oops, maybe not the best example. I don't like how he never reached forty. But you get the point.

"You are *not* wearing that out of this office. Period."

"We got a dress code?"

"Mr. Simet, would you like to explain to Mr. James why he isn't wearing that noose around my school?"

"My next success explaining something to Mr. James will be my first," Mr. S says. "Go right ahead."

"So you're going to side with him? The one thing you've never understood as a teacher—"

We may be closing in on that exploding bean. CHS is awash with rumors about the War Between Mr. S and The Bean.

"Maybe you'd like Marcus to wait in the outer office while we discuss this," Mr. S says.

Mr. S

Boy, some kids come and go, and some get into your gut. Not much you can do about it but hang with them and try to walk them through. Take Marcus James. The boy's got an IQ through the roof. But he's black in a school where that makes him a minority of one, and he's openly gay—in the sense that he doesn't deny it—which puts him in even rarer air, and he's in your face. He's extremely well-read for a high schooler, and vocal about what he reads, which doesn't make him a favorite with some of his teachers, particularly those who are *not* extremely well-read. If those aren't enough identifying characteristics, he swims open water in the lake to "keep his head on right." A gay, black, open-water-swimming Einstein. Tell me the universe doesn't have a sense of humor.

Now somebody's hung a noose on his locker, and I'm face-to-face with Principal Andrew Bean, considering whether or not I should make a case for letting him wear it.

"I need your backing on this, John," Andy says. "Don't let this be an issue you fight me on. You won't win."

"Can't let this one be about you and me," I say,

raising my hands in mock surrender. "What do you plan to do about it?"

"I'm going to confiscate and destroy it," Andy says. "Then we're going to keep our ears open to see if we can discover who perpetrated this . . . *act*, and see that they're duly punished."

If you play your cards right, you *can* get through to Andy. He and I have had some famous rifts, and I'm as opinionated as he is, but middle ground exists. He wants to do right by the kids, but he'll protect the reputation of the school above all else. One parent challenges a book over in the English department, and Andy is there immediately, leafing through every book by that author in an attempt to discover ahead of time which one will pop out of the stacks and bite him in the ass. He seems scared or defensive most of the time, but there's a teaching moment with this noose.

It won't be an easy sell; he wants it to disappear. "And after the noose is destroyed, who do you think is going to whisper the names of the culprits into our eager ears?" I ask him. "Sorry, Andy, this has 'gridiron heroes' written all over it."

"Don't jump to conclusions. We can't come out pointing fingers."

"Maybe not, but I don't have to bring you up to

date on nooses in this country's history, right? This will bring bad publicity if we don't handle it right."

"I'm not an idiot, Simet."

That remains to be seen. "You remember the Jena Six."

"You're not going to compare this with *that*. This is completely different."

"Let's see," I say, "some racist kid or kids hang a noose on a black kid's locker here. In Jena, they hung three nooses from a tree. Here they made the noose pink to make sure they covered *all* their bases. If I were an English teacher, which I once was, I might see a *theme* of bigotry and hatred."

"The larger point," Andy says right back through slightly gritted teeth, "is that Jena is in the heart of Louisiana, where racism has a long and colorful history, if you'll pardon the pun. The tension there goes back pre-Civil War. We live, if you haven't noticed, in the Northwest. Our school has one African-American student, who also happens to be gay and a little on the loud side, and who doesn't have the good sense to keep below the radar; he flaunts his intellect at every turn. I know this place is more conservative than you'd like, Simet, but it is not the Deep South and we are not going to have a racial 'incident.' It's a jock culture, and while

I agree jocks can be pretty single-minded, that's not all bad. Now I don't agree with someone hanging a noose on an African-American kid's locker, but this is going to be *over*."

"What about the fact that the noose is pink?"

"Are you sure you want to go there?"

"Excuse me?"

"It is not lost on me, John, that you are not married, have no children, and I have never seen you out with a woman."

Jesus. "Have you ever seen me out with a man?"

"No, of course not."

"Has it occurred to you that maybe you haven't seen me out with *anybody* because I'd never take anyone someplace you might be, so I wouldn't have to claim I know you?" I *have* to stop letting him piss me off. I'm not offended by his observation; there's certainly nothing wrong with being gay, and if I were, I assume I'd be matter-of-fact about it. I'm offended that he's looking for a diversion.

He reddens.

"Whether I'm gay or straight, Andy, I'm not embarrassed about who I am, so you're damned right I want to go there." Andy will tell you over and over that he holds nothing against any man or woman due to race, creed, color, or sexual preference, but with guys like Andy Bean you turn down the sound and watch the picture.

"I'll say it again: we're not going to make this bigger than it is. It's a prank, and we'll get to the bottom of it if we can, but this does not escalate. Do you understand?"

"I understand, but don't confuse my understanding with agreement. Look, Andy, I'm all for turning the best face of education out for the public, but it has to be a real face. You know, my dad came up in the sixties, and while he was quick to talk of the progress made in civil rights, he was every bit as quick to talk of the distance yet to go. We're well into the twenty-first century, and *nooses* are still dropping down. Conservative or not, single-minded or not, you don't call a noose of any color a prank."

The Bean moves to the chair behind his desk, as if the shiny oak between us gives him status. "I was told you were hired against the better judgment of some board members, and I'll bet this is a reason. Your work history shows troublesome conflicts; you've always been so quick to side with students against school authority. I'm guessing if it hadn't been midterm and the school hadn't been in such a pinch, you and I might not be having this conversation."

"But it was and you were and we are. Does the word

tenure mean anything to you? Andy, do you know what I'd do in Marcus's shoes?"

"You had *better not* give that boy ideas."

"That *boy's* IQ is upward of 160. He's forgotten more ideas than I've had. And the term 'boy' has a similar history to the noose." God, it's so easy to get into it with Andy. He makes it fun.

"John, you know as well as I do this school can't afford negative publicity right now. We're trying to pass a levy at a time when the community isn't exactly happy with our overall performance."

"Maybe we should perform better. Look, I won't push Marcus one way or the other, but when I was his age, I would either have witnessed total outrage by administration and staff in the face of this, or I'd have brought down the house."

"Excuse me?"

"TV. Newspaper. Hell, carrier pigeons, if that's what it took."

"Don't you do this, Simet."

"I'm telling you what I'd have done. The administration and the law tried to bully the black kids in Jena, and suddenly they were face-to-face with Jesse Jackson and Al Sharpton and CNN, as they should have been. Jesse Jackson has Verizon, and so does Marcus. It wouldn't cost him a cent to make that call."

"How in the world would you know if Jesse Jackson has Verizon?"

"He advertises it on TV." Hey, so I'm prone to exaggeration. I have no idea whether or not Jesse Jackson has Verizon, though I know he doesn't advertise it on TV. But there's a point to be made, and I'll bet Jesse is willing to let me stretch the truth.

"Simet, if any teacher has the inside track on Marcus James, you do. I'm asking you to help take the heat out of this." He pinches the bridge of his nose. "I swear I'll have your job if you turn this into a circus. You may have tenure, but if your behavior actively damages the school or its reputation, you *can* be fired."

I can't tell if I scared him with visions of what *my* adolescent take on this would have been, or with Jesse Jackson on Verizon, but the stakes have been upped. Left to my own devices, we'd have Marshall and Stone and Strickland in the office under bright lights until they cracked, and none of them would play another down of football until they were on a team with Adam Sandler and Chris Rock. But I'll follow Marcus's lead. He's in a minority of one, and he needs to get to wherever that fabulous mind takes him—via Stanford University—in one piece. Roger Marshall's uncle is in jail for murder, and at least a part of the motive for his crime was race related. That family is no fun. "Look," I say. "I don't know what Marcus has in mind, and I'm leaving it up to him. Maybe if we bring him back, you can compromise with him."

Andy is exasperated; feels his control slipping away. I've seen him in this state before. In fact, some of my prouder moments have occurred when I've put him in this state.

He opens the door to find Marcus tightening the noose as he goes cross-eyed and sticks out his tongue. Methinks he has his work cut out for him.

Marcus

So The Bean pretends he doesn't see me stringing myself up in the outer office and invites me back into the inner sanctum, and for a second he seems all better. But when The Bean pretends he doesn't see something, pay attention. The Bean sees all.

"Marcus," he says. "How can we get this resolved?"

"Find the guys who did it and throw 'em out of school."

The Bean blanches. Wow. I was just startin' high. You know, tell 'em you want ten thousand shiny ones for your Hank Aaron rookie card, and see what it comes to. No matter anyway. O.J.'s got a better chance of finding his dead ex-wife's killer on a golf course than these guys have of finding their hangmen, and for the same reason.

"It's difficult to get fingerprints from a rope," The Bean says. "Practically impossible. You need a smooth surface to get the print."

"Yeah," I say. "Plus, I been checking this thing out pretty good; you know, for authenticity. So if you get prints, you'll probably have to expel *me*. You were an

English teacher in your former life, right, Mr. S? Isn't that an example of *irony?*"

Mr. S says, "It is indeed, Marcus."

"Well, I can't promise to find the culprits and throw them out of school," The Bean says, "but I can promise we'll try to get to the bottom of this one way or the other. I'd need you to give me some time."

"Take all the time you need, sir," I tell him, feeling all charitable an' shit because I thought he was going to ream me good. Mr. S must've worked some voodoo here. "I'll just wear this till we come up with a plan, jus' so the whole thing doesn't get all old and stale. And forgotten."

The Bean is perplexed. I think I see a certain subtle look in his eye, one I've seen a lot in my life. Kind of a . . . what can I call it . . . an "I hate your queer black ass" look.

"There's simply no way I can let you do that, Marcus. If you walk into Ms. Ruth's class wearing that thing, I'll have to call a medic. And Mr. Grant wouldn't let you in the door."

"I've got an A going in Grant's class," I tell him. "I could take a few zeros and still pull a C. I'm sure you'll find the bad guys before I tank it."

The Bean sucks air.

"Jus' kiddin', man. Don't be thinking I'm all unreasonable. Tell you what. I'll just wear it in Mr. S's class. We're doin' First Amendment in there. It'll take some of the focus off those books you-all want to ban. It's win-win, I'm telling you." Before The Bean can answer, I say, "And I think I can speed up your search for the bad guys."

"How is that?"

"Start with the guy whose family's got a rebel flag painted on one whole side of their barn."

"Now tell me those weren't some pretty good negotiating skills," I say to Mr. S as he leads me toward his room by the noose.

"*Really* good negotiation skills," he says, "have to be effective in the *long* run."

"Well, I established my basic premise, like you taught me."

"Yeah, he knows you won't let this slide."

We walk into Mr. S's empty room. Prep period. I'm supposed to be in Grant's AP Calc class, but Mr. S can write me a pass. Grant is out of his depth in anything tougher than long division with remainders, and he hates it when I know shit he doesn't. Swear to God he'd give me an A+ to stay out of there.

"Your basic premise was perfect, but you were debating The Bean. I'll deny I said it if it leaves this room, but he's not exactly Daniel Webster."

"Man, I was feelin' so good. Who's Daniel Webster?"

"He was a good debater. This is a train wreck, Marcus. Even if Bean were committed to getting to the bottom of this, without a witness there's no proof of anything. You're going to wear the noose and Marshall and his henchmen are going to mess with you and it will escalate. You're aware, I hope, that Marshall's uncle is in jail for a hate killing, and there's not a member of his extended family who doesn't believe he was railroaded. I'll do what I can, but you be smart. Those guys are ballplayers, and that's worth a lot more second chances in the principal's office than you'll ever get. Let's stay awake."

I like Mr. S 'cause he'll tell you what's so even if it would get him in hot water with the boss man. I slip the noose off and hand it to him for safekeeping. I know he's saying truth. Marshall's uncle shot T.J. Jones's adoptive dad down at Hoopfest in Spokane a few years back because of a bunch of racial shit that went on for about a year. T.J. was the last black kid to negotiate these halls. If you believe the local historians, things changed for a while after that; folks preachin' brotherly love and shit, but then it fades, and guys like Marshall and Stone start rewriting that history, and pretty soon, if you listen to them, it was T.J.'s fault his dad got shot. You know, bein' "of color" and all. Those short-term memories are like waves lapping up over footprints on the beach. Real quick the sand is smooth again, and however things were is how they are.

"There's a principle to stand on," Mr. S says, "and I'll stand with you, but there won't be great numbers standing with us. There are plenty of kids and plenty of teachers, too, who are gonna hate it when they hear that noose was hung on your locker, but not many of them will be willing to do more than say it sucks and condemn whatever anonymous turdhead did it. They'll call it a prank and, if it doesn't happen again, let it fade. There's not much room to make something happen here. Bigotry turns ugly quick. I don't have to tell you that."

He looks at me long and hard. "A noose, pink or any other color, hanging on your locker is to be taken seriously. I don't know your family's personal history, but any black man in this country pays attention to that."

"In my personal history," I tell him, "I can run right down the line on my momma's *or* my daddy's side and find a hanging before I get three generations."

"Okay then."

I can't help but feel scared, listening to Mr. S. This guy doesn't back down. If Mr. S is nervous, well, he's like your canary in the coal mine—if he stops breathing, haul ass. "Maybe we ought to call it good on the noose," I tell him. "Point made. Plus I got my new love life to focus on, and my college entrance essay. Maybe I got some great material here."

"New love life?"

"I'll tell you," I say, "but you got to keep it on the down low."

He puts his hand flat toward the floor. "The down low."

I take a big breath. "Not even the down low, Mr. S. We got to hit *mute* on this."

"Mute it is."

"Johnny Strickland."

"Aaron's brother?" Man, the blood drains out of Mr. S's face like gravity just got supersized.

"You want me to call a doctor, man?"

"For me or you?" he says.

Mr. S

You have to wonder how some people get their license to educate. We come to school this morning to The Bean's announcement, through the school's morning news anchors, that first period will be canceled for an all-school assembly. That's nine hundred kids in one gymnasium. While they're filling the gym, I'm hustling to The Bean's office. I meet him at the door. "Tell me this has nothing to do with Marcus."

"It has everything to do with Marcus," he says back. "You're right. We can't sweep this under the rug. Hanging a noose on an African-American child's locker is unthinkable. We have to bring it into focus for the entire school."

"What changed?"

"I called Dr. Nethercutt." Nethercutt is the school superintendent.

"Come on, Andy. Nethercutt is the one person in this community least likely to be offended by a noose on a black kid's locker, much less a pink noose on a gay black kid's locker. The guy would make Rush Limbaugh's

····
177

birthday a national holiday. You'll put Marcus in the sights of every bigot in this school."

"We'll be offering a reward," The Bean says, "for information leading to the identity of the culprit or culprits."

"And nobody will say shit, and Marcus will be hung out to dry. The only possible witnesses are other ballplayers, and none of them is going to rat out his captain."

"Maybe you should have thought about that earlier. Dr. Nethercutt decided James will not hold us hostage. As long as he wears the noose, or even threatens to wear the noose, we're in jeopardy for negative attention. It's a win-win, as young Marcus would say."

"So Nethercutt wants to deal with the problem in a way that gives us no chance to actually solve it."

"You can take it up with him if you'd like."

"Yeah, I'm the guy to change his mind." Dr. Nethercutt and I haven't seen eye to eye on an issue since my first day. He was a believer in No Child Left Behind, and I was a believer that no child was being left behind because no one was going anywhere. We were testing kids into comas. Higher-level education was out the window in favor of teaching to the test. My first all-district meeting ended in his threatening to put me on probation. I've been on probation since. I can mess around with The Bean and find middle ground once in a great while; Nethercutt's a whole different story. "Come on, Andy. There's no integrity in this. You guys are setting him up."

"I have to agree with Dr. Nethercutt on this one, John. Marcus made his bed."

"Marcus made his bed? Somebody hangs a noose on Marcus's locker and *he* made his bed? Jesus. And big surprise, by the way, that you agree with Nethercutt on this one. How would that make it different than any other one? You've got your nose—"

"I'd be careful, Simet. You're dancing close to insubordination."

Marcus and I share a personality trait I'd better rein in here—the one that gets us both in deeper than we should get. Plus, I'd better see if I can get Marcus out of that assembly. About ten things could happen, and nine of them are bad. "You guys are going to do what you do," I tell The Bean. "When the smoke clears, remember I said the point of no return was when you called this assembly."

Dr. Nethercutt should have been a politician. He stands center circle in the gymnasium, surrounded on three sides by the student body as if in a giant town hall meeting. The place is abuzz, because we don't get

Nethercutt here to rub shoulders with the masses unless some serious shit has hit the fan. I'm looking through the crowd for Marcus, who isn't hard to find in a sea of white faces, but he's too deep into the bleachers to get to him. At least he's not wearing the noose.

Then I see at least one reason why. Nethercutt holds it high.

"Ladies and gentlemen. Thank you for your time this morning."

Like we had a choice.

"How many of you know what this is?" He dangles the noose from his raised hand. It had been behind folders in my filing cabinet. Nethercutt went through my things to get it.

There are a couple of shouts of "Noose" and "It's a noose."

From the football section. "A *pink* noose!"

"That's right!" Nethercutt says into the mike. "It's a noose. And it was hanging on the locker of one of our students. Now I'm not going to mention the name of that student, because that's not what this is about. But this is a symbol. A symbol of hate. And I won't have that in my school."

I look for Marcus in the crowd, but he has slid down far enough as to be barely visible.

"I'm offering a seventy-five-dollar reward for anyone who can prove, beyond a shadow of a doubt, what culprit or culprits did this. Serious consequences will follow."

Nethercutt is offering seventy-five bucks. Jesus wept.

A figure steps out of the bleachers and strides toward him.

I lean over to The Bean, beaming beside me at Nethercutt's fortune-building offer. "That's Matt Miller. Kid's a stud wrestler."

"Yeah. State wrestling champ at one-sixty, and a heckuva student. Very devout. They don't come any better than Matt Miller."

Matt smiles and motions to Nethercutt for the mike, which is gladly given. Very devout. Great. I should keep my biases to myself, but I don't like bringing the wrath of God into this.

"Good morning. Most of you know me. I'm Matt Miller. Under different circumstances I follow that with 'and I've taken Jesus Christ as my Lord and Savior,' but I'm also a believer in the separation of church and state, so I'll forgo it. 'Course *that's* my way of getting to say it without saying it."

Marcus has slid completely out of sight.

"Thanks for relinquishing the mike and this time, Dr. Nethercutt." He looks at the mike. "You may be about to have second thoughts."

Nethercutt appears taken off guard, moves toward Miller, but Matt turns slightly, shielding the mike from his reach.

"Our superintendent just offered maybe three tanks of gas to entice one of our gridiron superstars to rat out his buddies. Of course he knows that anyone who takes him up on it wouldn't live to fill the second tank. If you ask me, this is a good way for our school administration to make a show of addressing the problem while at the same time making sure no resolution is reached."

Whoa! Couldn't have said it better. Nethercutt has left the noose on the podium; Miller picks it up. Nethercutt demands the mike, moves threateningly, but Matt Miller is a state champion wrestler. In his state championship match last year, he was taken down only twice, and made lightning escapes both times. "Begging your indulgence, sir. I'm not finished."

"Oh, yes, you are."

Matt smiles. "No, I'm not."

Nethercutt lunges for the mike, and Matt dances easily out of his reach. Nethercutt straightens his suit jacket. "Mr. Miller, I am the superintendent of this school district. I'm demanding that you hand over that mike."

Matt says, "Dr. Nethercutt, I'm a solid three-six grade-point-average student who has earned a state wrestling championship for my school, and I will give you the mike as soon as I'm finished, which won't be five minutes."

Nethercutt hollers for security.

This gym is quiet.

"Young man, your diploma is officially at risk."

"So be it."

Whew! This Christian has some *nuts*.

"As a man of God, I'm interested exclusively in the truth. Somebody in our student body hung a noose on an African-American student's locker." He stares at the noose in his hand. "And it's pink. Some asshole who doesn't know the origin of the phrase 'killing two birds with one stone' killed two birds with one stone. He, or they, also committed a hate crime."

Nethercutt stands with his hand out, flushed bright red.

"When I heard Dr. Nethercutt's spectacular reward offer, I asked myself something I ask probably five or six times a day: What would Jesus do? See, I know who put the noose on Marcus James's locker. Roger Marshall hung it, and Aaron Strickland and Ray Stone watched."

Roger Marshall stands up in the bleachers and yells,

"That's a goddam lie, Miller, and you know it. What're you, James's boyfriend? I'll see you after school!"

The Bean starts onto the floor, but I grip his shoulder. He glares at my hand, and I remove it. "There'll be news coverage," I whisper. "I'd think long and hard before making my next move."

"I'd love to see you after school," Miller continues. "If I heard you guys right, Strickland *tied* the knot, but I can't be sure I heard right." He turns back to Nethercutt. "I can't prove any of this. In a court, it's hearsay, because I was dressing down for a preseason workout in the locker room when I heard them laughing about it." He offers Nethercutt the mike. "I don't know what is to be done about it," he says, "but I just thought I should get the truth out. It's what Jesus would do."

I would like, at this point, to take back anything I ever thought about Very Devout Anything. Nethercutt snatches the mike, thumbs the off switch, and says something to Miller between gritted teeth. Miller smiles, pats him on the shoulder, and offers to shake his hand. Nethercutt sneers and turns toward the crowd, flips the mike back on. "What Mr. Miller just did was irresponsible. I want you to disregard it. I assure you all, we'll look into this and it will be handled appropriately. You may return to your classes now."

Marcus

Holy shit! I came to school this morning all willing to let the noose hang in midair in Mr. S's room and just watch what kind of bad mojo it gathered. I told my granddad about it last night, and he looked at me with those big sad eyes of his and said, "You do what you got to do, boy—you always do—but don't go bitin' off more than y'all can chew. You be sure somebody's got your back, or you lay low. Them Marshalls is mean as snakes."

Plus, I got Mr. S's point; you choose the time and place to make your stand. All I got to do is lay low and get my ass to Stanford, which was my new plan after talking to my grandpops. But then Nethercutt calls me out. Got to hand it to him; he did what I did, opened the situation right up. See, when I put that noose around my neck and walk into class, it's like saying, "Bring it." Shee. Everyone knows where it came from. I been in the South, all the time seein' pickups; two big ol' rebel flags flyin' straight back in the eighty-mile-an-hour wind created by the third-grade-educated rebels speedin' down the freeway. You know to stay away from *those* dumb bastards; they got a *mandate* to shoot you. And I've read about Kansas; I know anybody wearin' a cowboy hat drivin' his family in a Taurus up to the Holy Church of Jesus Christ is probably not a good candidate to hear how good his muscular buttocks look in those jeans. There are things you expect in certain parts of the country. But see, you could be wrong. The guy in the pickup *could* be just livin' out his family history; he read some bullshit American History textbook and came away thinking the Civil War was *really* fought between the industrial North and the agricultural South over economy and his ancestors weren't racial bigots and they maybe even died heroically in it. You might talk that guy right out of his hate. And the guy in the cowboy hat *could* be headed to the church to tell the pastor that he and his family are scoutin' out other churches 'cause they can't hang with a congregation that feels gays are an abomination, 'cause one of his kids *is* gay. All that *could be*. But if you live in the northwest part of the United States of America, which didn't even have a part in the Civil War, and your family has a rebel flag painted all up one side of your barn so you can see it five miles away, and your uncle wears a different color T-shirt every day that says ONE MAN, ONE WOMAN, ONE MARRIAGE UNDER GOD, well, let's just say that stacks the deck pretty good against a Marcus James getting invited to dinner at *your* house unless he *is* dinner.

So laying low wasn't a bad idea. But Nethercutt aimed every eye in the student body at me, and Matt Miller locked them all in, though Miller's intent was good, and he may have made me a little bit safer calling Marshall and his buddies out. Something bad happens to me after all that, those guys will fall into the category of "persons of interest." But all in all, it feels less safe around here than it did, say, this time last week.

"Teachers. Please excuse the interruption. Would you send Roger Marshall, Matt Miller, Aaron Strickland, Ray Stone, and Marcus James to Mr. Bean's office immediately. Thank you."

Shit. I'm a smartass and I stand up for myself when I can, but I do not look forward to walking into that particular mix of inhumanity, especially with The Bean and Nethercutt running things. So I'm hauling down the hall, trying to get there first; you know, pee in the corners and establish my territory.

"Mr. James. Good to see you." The Bean.

"Wish I could say the same, sir," I tell him. No territory to establish; I'm dead last. Marshall and his guys stare at me like I just scored a touchdown for the other team. Man, how is this shit *my* fault? Matt Miller leans against The Bean's desk, arms folded, staring down the Marshall gang. Nethercutt is seated in the corner, jotting down some notes, and The Bean shuffles papers like a rookie dealer in Vegas. He clears his throat. "I don't know exactly where to start here. We've had an interesting couple of days. . . . "

"I know where to start, Mr. Bean, so why don't I do that?" Nethercutt stands. "I want this solved today, gentlemen, and it will be." He turns to Miller. "Mr. Miller, I don't appreciate the position you put me in at the assembly today."

"With all due respect, sir, I didn't put you in any position. I simply said what was true."

"Well, I didn't experience that due respect. You as much as said I didn't want to discover the source of this." He holds up the noose.

"You got all that was due from me," Miller says back, and I'm getting ready to dive under The Bean's desk. This wrestler boy's stayin' on the offense.

Nethercutt stares daggers at Miller, and that's *almost* not a metaphor. But Miller looks like you could stick daggers in him all day long and then he'd just stretch out and go to sleep.

"You had better watch your impulses, young man. That state wrestling championship will get you only so much, and I'm warning you, you've about maxed it out."

"Dr. Nethercutt, off the mat I don't do *anything* on impulse."

"Be that as it may," Nethercutt says. "In my opinion you fanned the flames of a potentially dangerous situation, and I'll tell you right now there may be consequences for that."

"If there are, there are, but you might want to remember my mother is a pretty good defense attorney," Miller says back.

"Are you threatening me?"

"Yeah, I guess."

Whoa!

Miller keeps talking. "Sir, I represent three entities when I act: God, my family, and my school. I'm comfortable that God backed me today, and so did my folks. I guess it remains to be seen what my school will do."

Marshall stifles a laugh. Neither Miller or Nethercutt even notice; they're eyeball to eyeball.

Nethercutt blinks. "Look, Matt, I'm trying to fend off a potentially volatile situation while at the same time keeping this school reflected in a positive light going into this bond issue, whatever it takes." He dangles the noose, turns to Marshall. "Mr. Marshall, tell me what you know about this."

"Not a thing, sir. Miller is lying. None of us knows what he's talking about."

Nethercutt looks back at Miller, who raises his eyebrows. "Hard to know who to believe, huh?" Miller says.

Nethercutt turns to me. "What about it, Mr. James? What has to happen for you to let this go?"

Just being around Miller makes a guy want to stand up and fight, but there's not a one of those ball players doesn't outweigh me by forty pounds. "I don't know," I say, "I came to school today thinkin' maybe I made my point. Next thing I know you're turning me into a marked man."

"I called that assembly to get to the bottom of this."

"Was that seventy-five comin' out of your pocket, or were you gonna get it out of petty cash?" I ask him. "I'll let the whole thing go right here if Marshall can turn his pockets inside out without double your reward offer falling out on the floor."

Nethercutt glances at Marshall. Marshall shakes his head.

"I'll ask again," Nethercutt says. "How can we wrap this up?"

I say, "You know what? I'm gonna give you this

one, Coach. I'm gonna take one for the mighty Wolverines. I don't want the football team to lose its big tough studly linebacker, 'cause I kinda like him in those tight pants, and I don't want the school to give up free lunches and art and music because we don't pass a levy. So I'm hangin' up my noose. I would ask a favor, however."

Nethercutt says, "Shoot."

"I'd appreciate it if today was the last day you figured out one more way to hold me up to the student body as the token faggot nigger."

The Bean leaps up. "Mr. James, I will *not* have that language in my office. You will apologize to Dr. Nethercutt, or I'll be sitting in this office with your grandfather negotiating your return to this school."

"I wouldn't advise that," I say back. "My granddad lays low, but you take him on over a noose and all y'all will be in the news." I like following this wrestling Jesus freak's lead.

"You listen—"

Nethercutt raises his hand. "Hold on, Andy. Mr. James made his point. I can handle the rough language. Let's get our house in order here." He turns to Miller. "Are you satisfied, Matt?"

Miller doesn't move; arms still folded, looking at the

floor. He shakes his head slowly. "Naw, I'm not satisfied. I don't think anyone has taken this seriously enough. As recently as 1969, this was openly a sundown town. That noose represents a whole bunch of what is wrong with this country. You and Mr. Bean don't get it. You don't understand that we're more diminished by racism than Marcus is. It doesn't cost us as much, but we're more diminished. I thought I'd see a little more integrity in my waning high school years. But it's Marcus's gig, so I'm with him. I'm not satisfied, but if nothing else happens, I'm willing to let it die." He looks straight at Marshall. "If anything else *does* happen, that noose is part of the history I'll bring to bear." He picks it up off The Bean's desk.

Roger Marshall glares at Miller, then at me, with the steely gaze of a cold-blooded killer, but it's pretty clear The Bean and Nethercutt prepped him, 'cause he says dick.

I slap my leg and jump up. "Well, I'm glad we had this little meeting, but this is more fun than I can stand. Gotta get me some lunch." And I take my leave.

Mr. S

"So are we flush?" I catch up with Marcus in the hallway.
"On to the next challenge?"

"We flush," he says. "Tell you what, though. Throw
my man Matthew Miller's nuts in the back of your pickup
and haul 'em down to the weigh station. School record,
I'm tellin' you. That boy's ninety-nine percent *sac*. Shit,
he barely knows me."

"I was impressed."

Marcus laughs. "You just caught his opening
act. You shoulda seen him in The Bean's office just
now. I hope he can take care of himself. Marshall
looked killer."

"Matt Miller won state at one-sixty. That makes him
a natural at one-seventy-one. Barring the use of weapons,
I think he can take care of himself."

Marcus shakes his head. "Well, let's hope they bar
the use of weapons. I gotta get to class. I feel like giving
more people fewer reasons to send my ass to see The
Bean for the next week or so."

Matt Miller

I hope *this* is as strange as the day gets. Guess I shouldn't complain. *I* decided to take Dr. Nethercutt on, but what choice did I have? WWJD, right? What would Jesus do? Well, Jesus *never* backed down. That's my standard, though I'll never approach His state of grace. Man, when I saw that noose . . . How can you live in this country, know its racial history, know its biases against colors and creeds and sexual preferences, and stay quiet when you see a noose hung on an African-American kid's locker? And it was *pink*. That's because James is gay. These guys don't even know what to hate first. I don't worry about James. He's a gay black kid in the inland Northwest, thirty-five miles from where the Reverend Butler had a neo-Nazi compound for more than thirty years, and he's made it this far. This isn't as much about him as it is about *us*. I've been taught acceptance since I was a little kid, in Sunday school and in regular school. I know about the sixties and the civil rights marches and Dr. Martin Luther King Jr. and Malcolm X. I know about Matthew Shepard. As much as I love my country—and I'm going to find a way to serve it as soon as I graduate—I know we are in no way as cool as we tell ourselves. Right here in my high school lifetime, some white kids hung nooses from a tree they claimed as theirs in a schoolyard in Jena, Louisiana, because a black kid sat under it. He didn't chop it down, or see how high he could pee on it; he *sat* under it. Even more recently, some college kids at George Fox University, a *Christian* university in Oregon, strung up a life-sized cardboard cutout of Barack Obama. A judge in Georgia put a black, future NCAA scholar-athlete in jail because he had consensual sex with his white girlfriend when he was over eighteen and she wasn't. And that's just our racial profile. Take a gander at our sexual preference profile. Back in the eighties when the AIDS epidemic broke out, our government did squat for years, because guess who they thought contracted the disease. Gay men. And you know what the line was on that? It was a punishment from *God* for doing the nasty thing "within gender." If I'd been up and running when *that* crock was conventional wisdom, you'd have seen some serious *witnessing*. My God, we're coming to the end of the first decade of the twenty-first century and there are still people saying *their* marriages would be soiled if we let gay people be married. Like they aren't soiled by the fifty percent that don't make

....

it, or the others that stay together and hate each other. Shoot, if I were gay I wouldn't *want* to get married; I'd want to call it something else. Some TV preacher said the other day, "If we let gay people get married the next thing people will start wanting to marry is their pets. Where will it stop?"

Listen, people who want to marry their pets have already done to their pets what these guys are worried about. Wanting to marry an animal isn't about civil rights; it's about mental health. People just don't get it about Jesus. When He saw a wrong, He righted it. When He saw what wasn't His business, He left it the hell alone. I don't worry about Him wanting me to find a place in my heart for the Marcus Jameses of the world. That place exists naturally. Jesus didn't care whether you were some other color than pasty white, or whether or not you were gay. His Father made them and He loved them all. Jesus would want me to find a place in my heart for the Marshalls and the Stones and Stricklands, which, if you can't tell, I have a harder time doing, but at the same time He wouldn't want me to back off them when they did mean, stupid-ass things, because the thing Jesus loved as much as truth was justice. He'd want me to throw it in their faces so they could learn. This wasn't a guy looking through some book to find reasons to diminish others. This was a guy who'd have strapped on His steel-toed sandals and kicked some serious butt when He saw people like the Klan or these idiot neo-Nazis using His or His Father's name to spread their hate. Everybody's equal in the eyes of God. End of story. I got a plus in the Big Book today when I came out on the gym floor.

This isn't over. I don't like how my gut feels after the assembly and the meeting in Mr. Bean's office. Something is cooking. Marshall and his boys let it all go way too easily. That's why I backed off and let Marcus run with it. But my eyes are open; I stuck my nose in it, and I can't pretend to not know what I know if it hits the fan. Any time there's a Marshall involved, there's a better than fifty percent chance of trouble. Roger's uncle tried to kill his own stepdaughter several years ago because she was mixed race and he blamed her for his troubles. He ended up killing someone else, but what's stuck in my head is that his family still thinks *he* got screwed. Somebody needs to . . . oops, *that* was an un-Christian thought. I allow myself several of those a day.

Mr. S

When school is out today, I catch Marcus on the school lawn, carrying his Speedo workout bag to his car.

"Listen, buddy, would you mind if I drove out to your place and talked with your grandfather?"

"What'd I do?" he says with usual Marcus James exaggerated defensiveness.

"You're clean," I say, "but I think your gramps needs to know we're up to speed on this noose business and that at least some of us take it seriously."

"Man, one reason I let it drop was I didn't want to worry him. He'll think Marshall and the boys are fixin' to string me up for real."

"Just the same . . . "

"Yeah, man, okay. I don't care. But don't make it bigger'n it is. He worries about me too much as it is."

"Good for him. You headed for the lake?"

"Uh-huh. Only got another week or so of decent water temp. Then I got to bring it indoors. Hey, man, you're a history scholar. You know whether any black dudes swum the Channel yet?"

"The English Channel?"

"No, the Kenyan Channel. *Yeah*, the English Channel."

"I do not believe any black dudes or dudettes have swum the English Channel," I tell him, "but I will Google it while you're out there getting ready to."

"How about Rhodes scholars?"

"How *about* Rhodes scholars?"

"Swum the Channel."

"That would surprise me even more than black dudes," I tell him. "If you're smart enough to be a Rhodes scholar, you damn well better be smart enough to stay out of the English Channel."

"It's my destiny. The first black Rhodes scholar to swim the English Channel. I'm gonna be *so* famous."

I shake my head. "For a minute or two at least. And don't forget *gay*. It won't exactly make you Jackie Robinson."

"It will to English Channel swimmers," he says. "Listen, catch you later. I gotta get out there while I still got daylight. Tell my granddad I'm gonna be a little late, okay?"

"Done." I watch him walk toward his car, swinging his workout bag to the side and over his head, Will Rogers style, singing some rap song. The first gay black Rhodes scholar English Channel swimmer, and I knew him when.

■ ■ ■

"Yeah, he tol' me. Damn! What year *is* this?"

"I know, Wallace. I thought you should know he's not alone. Marcus didn't want to worry you more than you were already, but he decided it was okay if I came out. Good thing, 'cause I was comin' anyway."

"Sit down, I'll pour you somethin'll take the edge right off your day, teacher man."

"Sounds good." I take a seat at Wallace James's kitchen table.

He pours me a stiff Scotch, and one for himself. "Think there's more to come of it?"

"I don't think so. Another student called the Marshall kid out in an assembly, so he knows all eyes are on him. I'm gonna sit down with his coach and make sure we have him boxed in. If Coach Steensland knew for sure Marshall did it, he'd boot him off the team in a minute. Steensland's new here, and he's a good man; he'd knock that stuff down even if he knew it would cost his undefeated season."

"That's good to know. Come out to the garage. I got somethin' to show you."

In the garage, Wallace unlocks his toolbox and pulls out the wide, shallow bottom drawer, extracts a flat metal sign, and hands it to me. I read it aloud. "NIGGER

DON'T LET THE SUN SET ON YOUR ASS IN CUTTER. My God, Wallace, where did you get this?"

"Come with the house."

"What?"

"Guy who sold me the farm wanted me to know what I was getting into. They took this sign down . . . 1969, I believe. Had one near the city limits sign on both ends of town."

"1969? That's a year after the '68 Olympics."

Wallace looks at me like, *Duh!*

"Black athlete semi-boycott. Tommie Smith and John Carlos and the black fist. Martin Luther King Jr. had only been dead a year."

"I know. Ol' Mr. Bennett—he's the guy sold me this place—said Marshalls was a lot of the reason the signs were up in the first place. That boy's grampa was mayor. First couple years I was here, all kinda stuff got broke."

"So you are worried about Marcus."

"Been worried 'bout him since I moved in. He seems to get along okay. Got a big mouth on 'im, but he's kinda funny and that gets him by, I guess. I 'spect I'm beholden to you for keepin' an eye out for him."

"No beholden to it, Wallace. My pleasure. That kid keeps me on my toes. There's not much I teach he doesn't already know something about."

"Well," Wallace says. "I'll talk to him more about this noose business. When you've got enough support, you can make some noise, but if you don't, well, you better lay low."

"I'll back you up. Do you know if Marcus is dating anyone? He talk to you about that?"

Wallace looks embarrassed. "Oh, no. He don't talk to me about that kind of thing. Why you ask? Marcus spendin' time with someone? Got to tell you, Mr. Teacher Man, I never quite got it about the homosexual thing. Sometimes I worry more about that than the color of his skin. Can't very well keep folks from knowin' you're black, but that gay thing, I might woulda kept that under my hat. Give these boys jus' one target to shoot at."

Marcus

I wish I could tell people, like, you know, *articulate,* how it feels to get into the water and just start swimming. I wasn't kidding Mr. S when I said I wanted to be the first black dude to swim the Channel. 'Cept it's like twenty-six miles, and the farthest I've gone is maybe one and a half up in the lake. But it's calm and there's this *rhythm* and you can't hear anything but air comin' in and the bubbles goin' out. You have to be careful swimming in open water, because there are fishermen and water skiers and jet boaters out there and you do not want one of those things whackin' into you. So you're supposed to swim *with* somebody, and I've got this flag, which sticks up like a flag you put on the back of your bike when you want to get all visible. My gramps made it from one of those bicycle flags. Attached it to this plastic belt. It doesn't weigh anything, but it sticks up and says there's a flesh-and-blood human right under it and please don't run your motorboat over him. I don't swim with somebody because, like, who would I get? There aren't a lot of channel-swimmers-in-training lined up. I use the flag, but that's a mixed blessing because while it keeps unsuspecting drunk watersportsmen and -women from running over me accidentally, it tells guys like Roger Marshall where I am, and they can come kill me on purpose. On a number of occasions they've circled me at high speeds, creatin' some surf. Those boys are creative. But I'm safe now, because soon as I get in my car I'm headed for the lake and in about fifteen minutes they'll be headed for the football field.

"James."

Shit. It's Strickland. "What?"

"Com'ere."

"In a hurry, man. Got to get up to the lake."

"The lake'll still be there in five minutes. Come over here."

Motherfucker. None of these guys ever have anything to say I want to hear. Some racial bullshit, or some stupid threat.

I walk over to his car.

"Rog has a message for you."

"Lemme guess. He wants me to be an honorary member of the Letterman's Club. Love to, but I really don't have time—"

"He's inviting you to shut your fucking mouth about

that noose. Let it die so you don't have to."

"I didn't say anything about the noose. I just wore it. Miller's the guy said you guys did it. If I can't stop y'all from riding me, how am I gonna control Matt Miller?"

Strickland reaches through the side window and grabs my shirt, pulls me in close. "Any bad shit happens to us, some *real* bad shit will happen to you."

I stare straight, past the side of his head.

"You understand?"

I keep right on staring. One of these days I'm gonna get tired of "managing" how I feel right now and give one of these guys a surprise. Fuckers always get you alone.

"I'll take your silence as that you do." He releases his grip. I fight the urge to tell him he could get into community college one day if he learned that the word for "that you do" is assent.

Matt Miller

If I hadn't been so enamored of flexing my biblical scholarship muscle, I might have saved him. I was planning to run partway around the reservoir after my weight-room workout, but I got waylaid by the BattleCry kids. BattleCry is this organization of aggressive Christians who think they need to define the moral high ground for teenagers who aren't them. They think it's a sin to have sex if you're not married, or if you're gay, so they're big on the abstinence-only approach to teenage pregnancy and even bigger into praying gay people straight. What the hell, at least they'll get a lot of practice. I wish God would get as sick of them as I am and just fire down a lightning bolt and yell, "Shut the hell up!" They have events that fill football stadiums, with Christian rock bands and nationally known Jesus freaks shouting out the Word. Tell you what, I'd follow Jesus into the eye of a hurricane, but saying "Christian rock" is like saying "Caucasian rap." Ain't no such thing. I'm a lot more Chris Rock then I am Christian rock, which is probably why I don't belong with these guys. I wish more people understood that spirituality is private. If you have to fill football stadiums and scream out your message all the time, you're not too confident in it.

At any rate, they missed the point of my "ministry" this morning in the gym, and as I trot out the front entrance headed for the lake, they cut me off.

"Hey, Matt."

"Hey, Darcy, what's up?"

"Could we talk with you for a minute?"

The closer I get to wrestling season, the more fiercely I train. I don't like to get caught even a little bit out of shape when I hit the mat for the first time. But I can shorten my run a mile or so to take time for Darcy Zindel, who is one beatific Christian, if you know what I mean. I say, "Sure."

"We're having an after-school meeting at Mike's," she says, nodding to Mike Campbell's house, just across the street. "Do you have a minute?"

I look down at my sweatshirt, which is doing the job for which it is named. "If you guys don't mind a little locker-room ambiance."

She smiles and I melt. "I think we can stand it."

I follow her and Charles Lott to the Campbell house, noting that they're holding hands, again giving myself leeway for two of those un-Christian thoughts: throwing

Charles into a quick takedown to make him ugly, and . . . well, I'll let you guess at number two.

Inside the house I think I've stumbled into the Marines of Rapture recruitment center. The honcho, Walt Johns, who I guess cries louder than the other BattleCriers, tells me right off what courage it took to stand up this morning. They too are committed to the truth, and they think it was great how I snuck in the blurb for Jesus. They too think what happened to Marcus was a sin; that there is no room in the kingdom of Heaven for that kind of hate, and though they're committed to get him to a center for scaring the queer out of him (my words, not theirs), they love him and would I like to join BattleCry because I'd be a strong voice for the Lord.

In a word, "Nope. Thanks, seriously, but not my thing. God created us all: black, white, gay, Down Syndrome, left-handers, deaf, blind, and control freaks."

We have a short conversation in which we discuss whether or not being homosexual is a choice. Funny thing, not one of them can tell me when they made the choice to be heterosexual. So I say they might do better, and have fewer people think they were nutballs, to get a sense of who the real Jesus was, tell Darcy if she ever comes to her senses she can find me in the wrestling room, and hit the road. Can't have taken more than maybe a half hour to forty-five minutes total.

By the time I get to the reservoir, Marcus James is dead.

Mr. S

Hindsight's twenty-twenty, as they say; maybe I should have done it differently. The smart thing seemed to be to go to Coach Steensland. He's a young guy, but a hard-ass old school football coach on the field, and a guy who knows that only a small percentage of the guys who play for him will ever go on to play in college or beyond. He wants them to lead responsible, productive, well-educated lives. He's a twenty-seven-year-old throwback, and it doesn't take a genius to see why his kids play so hard for him.

"The Miller kid is rock solid," he said to me in his office before practice. "I've tried to get him on the football field, but he's single-minded. A wrestler first, last and always. What he said isn't proof Marshall did it, but I can't see him coming out of left field with his accusations this morning."

"I don't know him as well as you do, Coach, but I get the same sense. And your boys were pretty cavalier when Marcus showed up in class wearing the damn thing around his neck. Kind of a 'You know we did it and we know we did it.'"

"Gotta cut this off quick," Coach said. "I'm calling a meeting with the boys before we hit the field. I don't want this to blow up and we're all sitting around afterward wondering if there was something we could have done."

He asked me to wait in his office and headed for the locker room. When he came back I could have taken his pulse from across the room. "By God, those boys are going to grow up or they won't play another down for me!" He threw his cap into his chair.

I waited. There's a reason his players don't mess with him.

"Damn it!"

"What happened?"

He took a deep breath. "The same damn thing that happened in your classroom," he said. "They blew it off, laughed until I lowered the boom. I told them I know they did it. Claimed they didn't but it was with a wink, like, 'No big deal, huh, Coach?' I suspended them until further notice."

"Whoa."

"Marshall started to come unglued so I threatened him. By God, Simet, I don't know where these kids get their ideas. Football is a *game*, it's not a damned entitlement. They know that from day one if they play for me, but the other students treat 'em like gods and they start winnin' and it goes to their heads. Well, it is *not* happening that way on my watch." He walked to the office window and stared into the empty gymnasium.

"You can only do so much, Coach," I said. "You aren't their parent."

"I guess," he said. "Listen, I've got to get onto the field. I've got a game to win this Friday, and I may have to do it without three of my best players. I'll sit down with them and their folks tonight, and we'll get to the bottom of this."

I did *not* envy Coach having to sit down with any Marshalls. They've been staples of Cutter football for more than a decade. Most people around here can't remember a three-year stretch when there wasn't a Marshall on the team. And always a stud. Way I see it, nothing that happens on a football field could hurt worse than what happens in their house if they fuck up with the old man.

But Coach did not have to make that call.

My classroom phone rings. I set aside the papers I'm grading and glance at my watch: 5:21. Who would think I'd still be here this late? I'm famous for being the first teacher out of the parking lot after the last bell.

"Simet."

"Mr. Simet. God I'm glad I caught you. Could you come up to the lake? By the boat landing? Hurry." The voice sounds shaky, urgent.

"Who is this?"

"It's Matt Miller, sir. Please get here quick."

Ambulance lights flash as I crest the slight rise on the north end of town. A stretcher, Wallace James, Matt Miller, three paramedics, and a blood-soaked sheet covering the stretcher. Several yards away, Randy Mix, a city policeman, questions the Marshall gang. I slam on the brakes, leave the engine running, and sprint toward the loading dock. Wallace has gathered the blood-soaked sheet covering what I know has to be Marcus in his arms, and his back heaves with sobs. "Where's the flag? Where's the flag?" Matt kneels beside him, a hand in the middle of Wallace's back.

I grip Matt's elbow, pull him just out of earshot. "What happened?"

"Run over by a boat," Matt says, nodding toward the police questioning Marshall, Stone, and Strickland. "Propeller-blade cuts all up his legs and back. The paramedic says he's not sure if Marcus bled to death or if the prop cut his spine." The three are animated, stricken, shaking heads, stomping feet. Strickland's covers his face with his hands, yelling, "No! No! Oh, God! No!

We didn't see him! I swear, we didn't see him!"

"Those bastards killed him," Matt says. "No coincidences, Mr. Simet. No accident. You know it. They killed him."

"Don't jump to conclusions, son," I say. "You stand here and listen to what they say. I need to see if I can help Wallace."

There is no help for Marcus's grandfather. He is inconsolable, sobbing against the bloody sheet, saying his grandson's name over and over. I can barely breathe.

The paramedics put Marcus's body into the back of their truck, and I help Wallace in. "You need me to come, Wallace?"

He shakes his head, leans on the boat. "I don't need nothin' no more."

The paramedic van rolls slowly over the hill; no light, no siren.

Matt Miller and I stand and watch it go, both listening to the police finish up with Marshall and his buddies. It was Marshall's boat, he was driving. "Coach let us out early from practice," Marshall says, "so we come up here to do a little fishing. Strick got this new rod and we just wanted to try it out. Swear to God, it was like we said. Fished the cove down there south of the park. Nothin' was bitin', so we was headed over across. Thought I hit a log an' it killed the engine. Looked back and didn't see nothing, so I cranked 'er up and we headed for the other side. Swear we didn't even know we hit him till you stopped us when we was loadin' the boat. It was an accident, Randy. Man, I feel awful."

Randy Mix reads his notes, looks at the boys. Ray Stone stands with no expression on his face, his hair soaked; Strickland looks distraught, pacing back and forth, shaking his head and murmuring, "No. God *damn*."

Randy glances at the water. "Swear you couldn't see him, huh? I guess I can understand that; flat in the water." He looks up toward the hill. "I saw him from the road, but I guess I was higher."

"Swear to God," Marshall says. "I didn't see him till . . . well, I mean I didn't see him."

Matt says to me, "Those guys killed him, Mr. Simet. No other way this happens."

"Did he tell the cop a second ago that Coach let them out of practice early? Did I hear that right?" Miller nods. "Yeah, I think so."

"Well, he's told at least one lie. They were suspended."

Miller starts toward them, and I grip his shoulder. "Not yet. Let's see if we can find out what else they lied about. I know this feels bad, Matt. I can hardly breathe myself. But if we make accusations before we can prove them, these guys are going to walk away with a slap on the wrist."

"But there's no one else up here," he says. "Not another boat, nobody in the park. There are no witnesses."

I hold on to his shoulder, can almost feel the ache coming up from his heart. This kid is the real deal. "I see that. But all I have to do is look through my grade book to see that these guys aren't the next wave of Mensa. No way they're smart enough to cover all their tracks."

"Yeah," Matt says. "And either way, Marcus James is dead."

"Uh-huh. Marcus is gone."

Marcus James *is* gone. In a little under eight months, he'd have been home free, matching up that big brain of his with the professors at Stanford University, safe with his race and his sexual preference in the warm embrace of the Bay Area in Northern California. I consider the sign in Wallace's barn. NIGGER DON'T LET THE SUN SET ON YOUR ASS IN CUTTER. 1969. Well within my lifetime. I was nine. How could there be a sign at either end of town as late as that? Brown versus the

Board of Education was ruled on in 1954. The Civil Rights Bill was signed in 1963. And still it was 2008 before a black man ran for president on a major-party ticket. And he's *half*-black.

"Could I speak with Matt Miller?"

"This is Matt."

"Hey, Matt. John Simet. How are you doing?"

"Okay, I guess. Nah, I'm not doing okay. I'm going crazy. I can't think, can't sleep." I hear his voice crack.

"Me neither," I say. "Listen, Mr. Bean asked me a strange question this afternoon, sometime after the meeting you all had in his office with Dr. Nethercutt. He said you called Cutter a sundown town. Is that right?"

"Yes, sir."

"What exactly is a sundown town?"

"Uh, it's usually a small town in the Midwest or the West that had a policy of not letting blacks live there. They had to be out before the sun went down. They had them for other races, too—like Chinese and stuff—but mostly it was blacks."

"How do you know about them? Is that a formal name?"

"Kind of. I read it in a book called that. *Sundown Towns*. The author is a sociologist. If I remember right, he wrote it partly because he couldn't figure out why there were so many all-white small towns spread around the country. Like, African-Americans were mostly slaves in the South, and it seemed to him like they'd go where there was agriculture. But most of them ended up in cities. You know, like, in ghettos. Not a natural place for them to have gravitated. So, like, this guy, the historian—his name is Loewen, I think—starts investigating. Finds out there were a bunch of towns, like hundreds and probably thousands, that had policies not to let blacks live there, or to let just one or two."

"Wow." I'm an American history teacher and I've never heard of this. I mean, I know blacks ended up in the cities; I know some moved West to do some cowboying right after the war, but this is news to me. "Remind me to get the title and author from you at school tomorrow, when I have a chance of remembering. And you're sure Cutter was a sundown town?"

"Yeah, he had it listed. He says in most of the towns, law enforcement would escort you right out to the city limits at dusk, if you were black. That is, if you were black and lucky. There were way more lynchings and beatings in the North and West than most people think."

"Listen, Matt. You going to be okay?"

"I don't know, sir. I can't find a place to put this. I

tried to eat tonight and I couldn't." He laughs, nearly devoid of humor. "I may have to wrestle at one-twenty-one this year."

"The only thing you can do right now is feel it," I tell him. "If you want to scream, scream. If you want to cry, cry. I'll be doing the same. You call if you need to."

"I don't know how I feel, Mr. Simet. I mean, I could cry and scream at the same time, and I gotta tell you, I'm so fucking mad I don't know if I can hold it in. Pardon the language."

"Don't pardon it," I say. "You have to be mad in the language you're mad in. Remember, call if you need to, whether you're sad or fucking mad."

"Thanks, Mr. Simet."

"Thank *you*."

"Yes, sir."

I snap my cell shut and stare into the dark of my living room. *Sundown Towns.* That was the sign Wallace showed me today. Interesting coincidence that he and Matt brought it to my attention within hours of each other, and within hours of a time when the sun would no longer set on Marcus James's ass at all.

Matt Miller

A boat prop coming up your back at thirty-five miles an hour will put three-to-five inch cuts all the way up. If it doesn't cut your spine in two, you'll bleed to death before anyone can close you up. I hope Marcus James didn't feel it. I hope the boat hit him and it was done. I can't close my eyes, because I keep seeing it, and I keep hearing his grandfather: "Where's the flag?"

It's too late in the year for there to have been anyone at the lake at that time of day. No witnesses will show; I know they won't. There are a few cabins along the shore, but most are summer homes; maybe two or three are year-round. Nobody came out of those two or three to watch when the ambulance came. If anyone had seen anything, they'd have come forth.

Man, what do you do when you know the truth, when it's stretched out in front of you, silent? I've been here in my room with my Bible all night long, reading passages, trying to find the answer. Saying the truth, searching for the truth, finding the truth are all over in this book. But I can't find anything that tells me what to do for myself when the truth taunts me. *Here I am in plain sight, and no one will (or wants to) see me.*

I'm sure this will end up in the "strange and mysterious ways" category where unanswerable questions go, but I can't accept that. If Mr. Simet is right, if those guys were suspended from the team because Coach Steensland thought they hung the noose, then they ran over Marcus to get even. Simple as that. Marshall's grandfather and his great-grandfather were both mayors of this town back in the sundown town days. They still have that stupid rebel flag on their barn. There is no one in their family who has even the slightest chance of stopping that nasty shit from rolling through their generations.

Roger Marshall is smart; he knew there were no other boats on the lake, so his had to be the one that hit Marcus, but he claimed it was an accident. Jesus, what was Marcus doing swimming without that flag? Wait a minute . . .

Mr. S

This is one of those days no teacher wants to live through. A school of nine hundred kids, and one of them is gone. Everyone feels mortal on this day. No way to explain it. A morning assembly. Bean and Nethercutt talk to the students; don't say anything more than that it happened. Tragic accident. A promising life cut short. Moment of silence. A couple of counselors from town have made themselves available in the office if anyone wants to stop by. After that, business as usual.

I went out to the James place late last night, after I talked with Matt, and sat with Wallace till morning; didn't see an ounce of bitterness toward the guys who did it. He was willing to accept they didn't see Marcus. Take them at their word. No point in ruining more lives than have already been ruined. "Don't know what to do," he said over and over. "Don't know if I can stay in this house without him coming home. I was preparin' myself for when he went to college, but then, see, he'd be comin' for Thanksgivin' and Christmas. I'd look forward to seein' him. Knew I was gonna be sad, but my grandson would be at *Stanford*. I got through eighth grade, Mr. Simet. Eighth grade, and my grandson was goin' to Stanford." Then he just slowly shook his head and stared.

"I know, Wallace. He was going to set the world on fire."

"Them cuts went deep, teacher man. Shoulda seen 'em. Damned boat sliced my boy open."

"I know, Wallace. I can't imagine."

"I seen it an' I can't imagine," he said back.

We must have gone through that conversation ten times. It all ended in the same place. He fell asleep on the tattered couch just before sunrise. I covered him with a blanket and came to school.

"Hey, Mr. Simet."

"Matthew Miller. Come in. Sit."

He sits at the desk directly in front of mine.

"Hear anything on the grapevine?"

He says, "Strickland found out Marcus and his brother were, like, boyfriends."

"What?"

"Yeah, when little bro got the news about the 'accident,' he broke down and spilled the beans. I guess he went psycho on Aaron, accused him of killing

Marcus on purpose. Ended up in the psych ward."

"Maybe some information will come out of that. Keep your ears open. Most people who commit a crime don't think of half the ways they can get caught. Bottom line will come when one or the other of them feels safer and starts talking."

"I don't even know if that would do it," Matt says. "I stopped by city hall on my way to school this morning. I know I shouldn't have, but I did. That Randy dude, the cop that questioned those guys at the lake, was just coming on duty. I flat told him I thought they ran over Marcus intentionally. He looked at me like I'd slept with his daughter and told me I'd best keep thoughts like that to myself. I asked him what would happen if I had proof. He grabs both my shoulders and stares me down; says, "Even if you think you have proof, you stay healthy keeping it to yourself."

"He said that?"

"Exact words."

"Sundown town, huh?"

Matt shakes his head. "You can take down the sign, but it's not as easy to take down the attitude."

Man, I wish I had this kid in my class. He's sharper than half the faculty, present company included. Sundown towns. Who'd a thought it?

The ache in my chest for Marcus won't go away. That kid was loaded with talent and personality. How far could he have gone? And how is Wallace going to survive? How do you put everything into your kid—or your kid's kid—and then watch it all bleed out through the cuts in his back? I've been a teacher all my adult life; a teacher and a coach. I've taught kids I've loved and I've taught kids I couldn't stand, but I've always been fair, I think, and I've always believed I treated them such that they got the benefit of the doubt from me. But that ended yesterday. I believe Marshall and Strickland and Stone ran over Marcus James intentionally, and I can't find any doubt to give them the benefit of. I want them caught, and I want them punished. We are coming to a place in this world where there is simply no more room for bigotry. We don't get any more chances, where we learn the lesson or we fail. No more retakes. No extra credit. It's one thing for a family like the Marshalls or the Stricklands to be ignorant and hold on to hate that goes back generations for whatever reason. But when Matt said the *cop* told him to shut up; well, that institutionalizes the bigotry. Sundown towns be damned, it ain't gonna happen on my watch.

Matt Miller

It's after eight o'clock. Dark. The time of day I like best to run. I'll have to start dropping major poundage soon, and I want to be in the best shape I can when the time comes. Plus, these runs are where I get right with the world. Something about the rhythm of my running shoes on the pavement or the hard dirt, the breathing in and breathing out, that sends power to my legs, makes me feel closer to my God. I talk to Him here. No church; no middleman. There's a time and place for that, a time for celebration in a crowd; but if I'm going to get it *right*, I get it right here, with the cold bright moon lighting my way.

I'm looking for some capacity for forgiveness that I can't find. Maybe I don't even know what it is. I have to find a way to forgive Marshall and his buddies. It's easy to want revenge, easy to go for it. It's easy to hate their stupidity and ignorance, their arrogance. See, forgiveness is easy when someone has wronged you by accident, when you're accommodating a mistake. That's no sweat, no test. The test comes when you find no redeeming qualities, when you know you're looking into the face of malice and in the end there will be nothing returned by the forgiven. You do it because it cleanses your heart. I have to forgive them so I can be clean in bringing them down.

I know what Mr. Simet said has to be right, that if you commit a crime a thousand things you never think of can go wrong. Smart guys *might* think of a third of these. That means the Marshall gang won't think of any. I run and let the pictures float through my head, like snapshots from the moment I crested the hill by the lake: the ambulance, the boat, Marshall and Strickland and Stone talking to the cop. Strickland pacing, looking all distraught, and maybe he was. He was pretty good at it. Stone's expression living up to his name. Something was off. It was Stone's wet hair. What was that about? His clothes weren't wet, but his hair was. Almost dripping.

"I remember that, I think," Mr. Simet says in the library before school. He's recording grades. "I'm not sure I put it together with anything, but you're right, it doesn't make sense.

"Yeah, he would have had to stick his head overboard, or get on his stomach and get it wet from the dock. What would be the point?"

"Keep asking yourself that until you get an answer," Mr. Simet says.

"I've got a detective's brain," I tell him. "When you read the Bible as much as I do, you have to ask yourself how some of that stuff got in there; like who put it, and what was the reason. If you don't get that down, you lose every argument with every nonbeliever, and that's a lot of arguments."

"Well, we're not dealing with intelligence of biblical proportions," he says. "So I'll give you a day to figure it out. And keep your head down."

In the hall, Darcy catches me by the arm. "I heard you were up at the lake when they brought Marcus James out."

I nod. "Yeah."

"We're having a vigil out on the lawn to pray for him," she says. "It would be nice if you came."

I'm hesitant. From what I know of Marcus James, he probably wasn't all that religious, but I guess there's less need to pray for someone who is; they've prayed plenty for themselves. The idea of a prayer vigil for him feels good, even though I'm not on message with these guys. Very possibly the fact that Darcy asked is the reason I'm going.

Just off the lawn at the side of the street, nearly twenty of us stand in a circle and join hands. Walt Johns leads the prayer. "Dear Lord, please take Marcus James into Your wondrous care. Most of us didn't know him that well, but he was on the precipice of his life, and it seems so surreal, so unjust that he's gone. But we know You work in ways we weren't meant to understand, and that his death has meaning, though it may not be clear to us. Forgive him, Lord, for his choice to go to the dark side with his sexual preferences, and forgive us for not being strong enough to help him find his way back. Had he stayed, we'd have found a way."

"And forgive Walt, Lord, for being left-handed," I say. "And forgive his parents for not tying his left hand behind his back, when he was making the decision to favor that evil hand." Everyone looks up as I drop the hand of the people on either side. "And forgive Darcy for her blue eyes, Lord. There *has* to be some way she could have made them brown." I turn to walk away.

Darcy says, "Matt, wait."

I raise my hands and keep walking, then turn. "One of you idiots go find a dictionary," I say through clenched teeth, "and look up the definition of bigotry. You all are giving this Christian thing a bad, bad name."

Christ. A kid eats it for seventeen years, gets mowed down by a motorboat full of thugs, then gets blamed. I just hope those people don't turn eighteen and vote.

But, it wasn't the rhythm of the road under my

running shoes that I needed to kick my detection attributes into gear. It was *temper.* In the middle of my anger at those jerks, it came clear. Stone's hair was wet because he was in the water. His clothes *weren't* wet because he took them off. But *why?* I suppose Marcus could have still been thrashing around and he got in to finish him off, but that sounds way out there even for one of those guys. It's one thing to run over a guy; it's another to deliver the final blow. That can't be it.

"Come in, Matt." Bean signals me into his office. "What can I do for you?"

"I need to go home."

He looks at me sympathetically. "I understand," he says. "It has to be tough. I hope you're not blaming yourself."

"Sir?"

"For your actions day before yesterday morning during the assembly."

"I don't understand."

"I just hope you're not thinking that set this all in motion."

I sit watching him. He *means* it. Just to be sure . . . "Set what in motion?"

"You know," he says. "Had Roger and his friends

been on the football field, they wouldn't have been at the lake and this awful accident would never have happened. They'd been suspended from the team. I thought you knew that."

"Yes, sir, I did know that, I just never thought to blame myself. Look, I just feel bad and I'm going home."

The Bean stiffens. "You mean you're here to ask permission."

"No, I'm leaving. I'll bring an excuse from home." I walk out.

In my mind I'm staring at a stone tablet. THOU SHALT NOT STEAL. Man, give me any one of those commandments and I'll give you a godly reason to break it. I'd kill to stop loved ones from being killed, or probably in a righteous war. I'd bear false witness in a second if it would keep someone I cared about out of harm's way. And on and on. I'm on private property and I'm about to break and enter, and I'll bet you I come out with some truth. See, that's what Jesus would do: go for truth.

I circle the house twice, finally get the courage to knock. I've got three Hershey bars with me, and if Mr. Marshall answers I'll try to sell them to him for a school fundraiser. I can guarantee he won't buy them, but I'll know whether or not he's at home.

No answer. Rang the bell twice and knocked once, hard. Unless he's in an upstairs bedroom with a rifle pointed at my temple, I'm pretty sure he's not here.

I circle the barn. The double front doors are locked by padlock, but I can see what I'm looking for through the crack between them. Several windows are broken and boarded over on the side of the barn that sports the Confederate flag, probably so the continuity of the image isn't broken up. Those Marshalls are picky when it comes to the images of their bigotry. I think I can knock a couple of boards loose to get in. I don't like being exposed to the road while committing my crime, but if I'm quick, no one will see me.

Inside, I see a rusty sign leaning against the far wall. NIGGER DON'T LET THE SUN SET ON YOUR ASS IN CUTTER. Nice. I move quickly to the boat, and on the floor just under the outboard motor, I find what I came for.

"Mr. Miller. I thought you went home for the day."

"I did, sir, but I'm suddenly feeling better."

Mr. Simet looks at his watch. "Might that have something to do with the fact that the school day has ended?"

He's pretty funny. So am I. "Actually I'm known as an eager student who values his education and knowledge in general. Wanna come out to my car and see what I found home-schooling myself today?"

"Love to."

At the car, I open the trunk.

"What is it?"

"The flag Marcus had around his waist in the water."

"Where did you get this?"

"Roger Marshall's boat. That's why Strickland's hair was wet. He had to get in and take the flag off Marcus. That's a cold-blooded son of a bitch."

He stares hard. "*How* did you get it?"

"I had to break a commandment; two, if you consider Marshall my neighbor. I coveted it, and I stole it."

He turns it over in his hands. "How do we prove it was there?"

"I took a picture on my cell phone. It has a time marker, which proves I took it before I brought it to you.

He says, "Let's go."

"I'd like to talk to whoever is investigating the Marcus James death," Mr. Simet says at the front desk.

"The black boy run over by the boat?"

You can see Mr. Simet's irritation. "Yeah, the black boy run over by the boat."

"I don't believe anyone's *investigating* it," the sergeant says. "There's no investigating an accident."

"What if there were evidence to the contrary?" Mr. Simet says.

"Depending on what it was, we'd take it under advisement. What do you have?"

"Pretty good evidence that the kids that hit him were lying about his visibility." Mr. Simet holds up the broken remains of the flag, with the piece of belt still attached. The sergeant reaches for it, and Mr. Simet hands it over. "Marcus wore it around his waist when he swam alone," I say, "so people could see him. The guys in the boat said Marcus wasn't wearing it when they hit him, that he was almost invisible. I was at the lake when they said it. They said it to an officer named Randy."

"Randy Mix," the sergeant says.

"That's him," Mr. Simet says.

"Randy's on duty right now. I'll give him a call on the radio. If he's busy I'll show it to him when he gets in. Let me mark it." The sergeant disappears down a hallway. In several minutes he returns, gets our names, addresses, and numbers. "We'll be in touch soon," he says. "Thank you both."

Mr. S

Man, how do I teach civics in Cutter High School? How do I talk to my students about justice and due process when I know damned good and well that a police officer destroyed evidence, lied to his superior's faces, and is out on patrol as I speak? How do I tell them a prosecutor gave Matt Miller and me twenty minutes before deciding he didn't have enough evidence to prosecute with nothing but a couple of blurry pictures from a cell phone of a flag in the bottom of a boat; a flag, he said, that *could* have been planted? He'd heard of the bad blood between Matt and the boys in the boat. It would all come down to he said, they said.

Matt, bless his heart, listened to the prosecutor, stood up, and said, "There's plenty here, sir, and you know it. But I see your heart plain as day, and I know I don't have a chance. So I'm leaving before I get any of you on me."

The prosecutor stood, red faced. "You smart-mouthed little prick. Don't you ever accuse me of shirking my duties. This case is unwinnable."

"Doesn't matter," Matt said. "The law requires you to stand up for the truth whether you can win or not. But I know you won't. Good day."

I walked with Matt to the door, felt his forearm trembling beneath his long sleeve. He turned at the door and pointed a finger at the prosecutor. "When you go to bed tonight, ask yourself this, sir. Ask yourself, when you're standing at the gates of Heaven, would you rather be there as the hater or the hated? There are just two sides to this. This shit gets paid." We walked to my car in silence, my hand in the middle of his back, knowing I was touching a young man who will approach greatness. When I let him off in the school parking lot, he walked to his car, started to unlock the door, and dropped to his knees, sobbing.

Tuesday afternoon, early November. Marcus hasn't been gone a week. I drive to Wallace James's place, park on the dirt road in front, and gather the courage to go in. A bluish light from the TV screen flickers. The rest of the house is dark. I knock, to no answer. Again. I try the door. Unlocked. I have to go in. I have to.

Wallace sits on his worn couch, staring at the television set, a half-full scotch glass sitting on the side table.

"Come on in, teacher man," he says. "Watch this with me."

Things have been so crazy around here I forgot what day this is, though I did make it to the polls. On the screen, a tall, young, handsome black man strides onto a stage with his family, a beautiful, confident wife and two smiling, waving kids. American flags stand like a fence line behind him. Tears stream down the faces of many of the tens of thousands of people in the park where he is about to accept his mandate as president of the United States.

I look over at Wallace; tears stream down his face, also. His watery eyes are glued to the small TV set. "Think if this woulda happened ten years ago, my boy would be alive?"

I watch the screen, and my heart swells with Wallace's. I'd rather be here with him than on the grass in that park in Chicago. Here, I can feel it personally. But . . . "Probably not, Wallace. The Marshalls are likely watching this over at their house right now, calling our new president a nigger."

"It's a start though," he says. "Maybe *twenty* years from now a kid like Marcus will live because someone steps up."

"A whole bunch of kids like Marcus will live, Wallace. You're right."

He gets up and walks to the kitchen, pours himself another scotch, and one for me, and we sit and watch the news for maybe an hour. There is triumph in the air, but far less triumph in this room. "Hell," Wallace says as he eases himself back onto the couch, "I don't even know what they got him for, 'cause he was black or 'cause he was gay. Been sittin' here wonderin' which way the hate was comin' from." He nods toward the TV. "Look at California. They was gonna let gay folks be married. Now they're gonna kill it. Word has it my people are helpin' to kill it." He shakes his head sadly. "I hope that's not true; it would mean a whole people, been kicked around all our lives, are votin' so another group gets kicked. Lordy."

"I think that's a rumor, Wallace," I say. "It isn't your people who are making that happen; it's just all those folks who can't stand to let people be different."

He stands. "You know, teacher man, bein' homosexual isn't somethin' my boy *chose*. He just was. Somebody's readin' the good book all wrong. You ask me, God creates it, God loves it. Simple as that. We got a ways to go."

They're replaying some of the new president's remarks. "Yeah, Wallace, but we just came a ways, too; right here tonight."

"What about that wrestler boy, he gonna be okay?"

"Yeah, I think so. He's not a wrestler boy anymore, though. When Coach Steensland said he wouldn't coach football if he had to take Marshall and his buddies back on the team, and the administration said he had to, he quit. Matt said he wouldn't wrestle for a school that celebrates murder."

"He's a gutsy kid. Wish he'd have known Marcus better."

"He knows him better now."

"I guess. I'm puttin' the place up, you know."

"For sale?"

"Yeah, I can't stand it. Can't walk from room to room 'spectin' to see him around the corner. Pretty sour on this town, too. I should be able to get enough for it to last out."

"Where'll you go?"

"Think I'll just go."

"Hey, Matt. How's it going?"

"Got some more offers to wrestle," he says, dropping three letters from major NCAA colleges on my desk. "Guess one state championship was enough. Screw The Bean. When I said I was hanging it up, he told me I was ruining my future. Man, I can hardly wait to get out of here."

"It has been a little toxic," I say.

"Yeah, toxic enough I'm losing my faith."

"Your religious faith?"

"I can't find a way to forgive those guys, Mr. Simet. That's one big test of a true Christian, the way I read it. I've said before, it's easy to forgive an accident, a lot harder to forgive malice. All I feel is hate. Right situation came up, I could kill those guys. I walk the halls hoping one of them will say the wrong thing. It's eating me up. I don't even know what forgiveness would feel like."

I'm afraid I can't help. I had those guys transferred out of my class because I couldn't stand to look at them either. But . . . "You know, before he left, Wallace told me something about forgiveness that's been haunting me; said he's been leaning on it."

"What."

"It's just a saying, really. Mark Twain. His wife used to say it before she died. Wallace's wife, not Mark's."

"What was it?"

"He said, 'Forgiveness is the scent the violet leaves on the heel that crushes it.'"

Matt runs that over in his head. "Whoa."

"Yeah. He said forgiveness was probably too big for most humans, that maybe we have to leave it to something bigger. Wallace was being eaten alive, just like you. He had some big-name lawyers ready to bring civil charges against the families of all three kids. I mean *big*-name lawyers."

"Why didn't he do it?"

"He said he didn't have the stomach to stay here and feel the way he feels," I tell him. "He said we all grow up thinking how our people taught us to think. That's Marshall's problem. But Wallace also said he was still mortified that when he first discovered Marcus was gay, he told him to leave; flew into a rage. Then he read about Matthew Shepard crucified on a fence outside Laramie, Wyoming, and he realized people get lynched because of hate, not just skin color. He said something else you would have liked. He said, 'I still got a little faith, teacher man. Those boys gonna live their lives however they live 'em, but when they get to the gates of Heaven, s'all gonna come out.'"

Matt smiles. "Yeah. Wouldn't matter to those guys whether or not I forgave them. Those fuckers are too mean to care. It's for me, but maybe Mr. Wallace is right. Maybe it's too big."

"Right. I'm not familiar with your specific beliefs, Matt, but I don't think humans are wired to forgive right away. In fact, for some things I don't know if they ever can. And I don't know that they should. That never made much sense to me. Twain may have had it right. It's the scent of the violet, the good that the wronged leave on their way out. The good the bad guys can't stomp out."

"May be."

"So finish your year. Get the grades, stay in shape. Go put all this to use."

Matt stands and hugs me, and I feel in the power of his arms why he wins on the mat. He waves with his back to me as he walks out the door.

Matt Miller

Meet me at the gates, Marcus James. You can walk me through.

NAK

Anger. All those stories. All that rage.

Anger drives a drunken man to push his beautiful three-year-old daughter's face against a hot wood stove, force her to live looking at life through the prism, and the prison, of those scars. Then, to a great extent, anger drives that burned, broken girl to fly.

Anger burrows deep into the soul to become hate and a promising young gay black man floats dead in a lake, his dreams finished. Done. Then it drives another young, talented man forward to tell the truth at any cost.

A girl and her father yell their angry words at each other so loud they forget they love each other.

Nak closes the door behind him, sits, kicks his feet up on the desktop, intertwines his fingers behind his head. For every story of angry destruction there is one of angry elevation. "Circles right around like a rattlesnake chasin' its tale," he murmurs. He thinks back to Hudge, the young impaired boy from all those years ago; the

victim of anger so mean it defied reason. "Wish I coulda
stuck a little anger into ol' Hudge's gut," he says again
to the empty room. "Powerful bit of rage mighta kept
that boy alive."

It feels so good to be back with the young ones, he
thinks. Watchin' them on the front end of things, with
a chance to manage it all. "Not a good chance, maybe.
But a chance."

All those stories.